Critical Acclaim for
"The Shapeshifter's Bride"

"GC Sinclaire is an amazing writer and master storyteller. Her writing is utterly captivating. I found myself immediately drawn into her characters and will long remember their adventures, but beyond that, I felt as though I had entered their world and had been there sharing in their exploits. I highly recommend this book to anyone wishing to engage in a fascinating adventure. Your journey will begin on the very first page!"

 Patton Boyle
Author of *Screaming Hawk, Screaming Hawk Returns,* and *The Peaceable Kingdom.*

"Fantasy and romance author, GC Sinclaire, yet again compels us to enter and participate in her magical story. Well-developed characters and intriguing plot lines capture the reader's imagination, and the vividly painted and bright images throughout the entire book will leave the reader definitely wanting more."

 John Blakemore
 Author

"With deceptive simplicity, GC Sinclaire's open and honest writing style first draws one into her character's life, and then into a world of magic and mystique. One soon discovers that all is not as it seems, and that there are deep secrets about the 'Old World' island retreat, into which Ella's thoughts and destiny have become intertwined."

 Robbi Baskin
Musician, Composer, and Teacher

"Critically acclaimed author GC Sinclaire has masterfully crafted an enchanting tale filled with magic, passion, and fantasy."

 Stacey E. Brown
 Teacher and Author

The Shapeshifter's Bride

A Love Story

The Shapeshifter's Bride

A Love Story

GC Sinclaire

Printed in the United States of America

GC Sinclaire
Gig Harbor, WA 98329
www.gcsinclaire.com

Publisher's Note: This is a work of fiction. Names, characters, places, and incidents are a product of the author's imagination. Locales and public names are sometimes used for atmospheric purposes. Any resemblance to actual people, living or dead, or to businesses, companies, events, institutions, or locales is completely coincidental.

The Shapeshifter's Bride/GC Sinclaire-- 1st ed.

Print Edition ISBN 978-0-9977915-8-7
E-Book Edition ISBN 978-0-9977915-9-4

Library of Congress Control Number:2019915962

Dedicated To:

**All my
Wonderful
Readers
And
The Divine**

Thank you!

Table of Contents

HOLY GRAIL

When a man loves a woman,
she is the most precious thing in his world.
He cannot help but say "I love you,"
be her hero, her knight in shining armor.
He will never give up on her,
and will work with her
to build something truly magical.
That man knows in his heart and soul,
he has no doubt that he has found:
His holy grail!

G C Sinclaire

September 2019

A Magical Change

Life can be heartbreaking. Sometimes doing what is right for oneself can be the hardest thing, as well as the most painful. Had I known then how much my life would change in just a few weeks, I would have made it through all that turmoil with a much lighter heart.

I had been so very in love with a man for many years but had to finally face the truth. There was no future, no security in the relationship. It was time to allow someone who truly loved me in my life.

I had such hope for Andrew and me. We had found our way back together several times in the past. We would get along really well for a while until old patterns reasserted themselves. Words and actions finally convinced me that this man did not truly love me and never would. At that point, I decided to make the right decision for myself. As I said, not easy, and I did miss him a lot. And, I could not help but wonder if my own fears had finally doomed us.

I had grown a lot in those years we were together. My quest to understand him, to remain positive and happy, had led me to a deeper comprehension of myself as well as the world around me. I saw a tremendous benefit in that and did not regret the time I had spent with Andrew, but it was time to let go and move on.

Another good thing that came of this heart-wrenching breakup was that my extended family and I drew closer together. I loved the way they were there to support me. Without them, I do not know how I could have survived those first few days when my heart and soul hurt so bad that I wanted to die.

❦

Let me introduce myself. I am Ella. Writer, all-around artist, adventurer, sailor, and a host of other things. I have a variety of talents, and I like learning, expanding my mind, and growing as a person. I am very spiritual, and I am a medium, which makes me fairly good at picking up on things.

I am blessed with keen insights and often have a sudden knowledge of things to come. I rely very heavily on my astute instincts and perceptions, and I treasure these gifts greatly. Without them, I would feel deaf, dumb, and blind.

And yes, before you ask. Knowing all that I do, how had I allowed myself to be hurt so deeply? I had sensed that there were buried issues in Andrew from the very first date but, being an optimist, had not expected for us to mirror each other to such a degree. My own hidden fears were triggered intensely by our relationship. I faced them and put them behind me because this was one lesson I did not intend to repeat.

I now had a much better idea what red flags to look out for, and I would never again permit myself to ignore them just because I was falling in love with someone. I had learned so much about men and dating due to all the research I had been doing in my effort to understand and thrive while living with Andrew.

❦

Time heals all wounds, they say. Yeah, right! Not in this case! It seemed the longer we were apart, the more I missed Andrew, and the more I hurt. This was beyond my understanding, but it had happened each time we had split up. It reminded me of a rubber band that stretched apart just to pull us together again!

I managed to hold my mind in check during the day, but nights were an entirely different story. To my great annoyance, Andrew kept sneaking into my dreams. I must have let go of him a hundred times a day, but somehow it never seemed to stick. I would wake up, and my very first thoughts were always of him. Longing for what could have been would fill my heart.

The grief I felt at the loss was intense. Despite all the reminders I had created for myself to make sure that I would stay away from him permanently, I started to forget the reasons I had left Andrew in the first place. Not even the words that had finally destroyed all my hope were enough armor anymore.

I did, however, remember the good parts vividly. Pictures of the places we had visited kept flashing through my mind. I had loved the adventures we had, the places we had traveled to in those years together.

⚜

My older brother saw my pain and struggle. He was the one most instrumental in helping me through the especially rough spots. He understood how I was feeling only too well due to his own experiences. Being the amazing person he is, he was always there for me. Richard lived an hour away, but he would drive over when things got really bad and just hold me so that I could allow my emotions free reign.

Finally, I had enough. I decided that the moment had come to put an end to this grieving process. Asking Andrew to get back together was not an option. I had been tolerating this heartache long enough. It was time to pull myself together. I was better than this! What made this one man so special that I would allow such misery in my life?

I think what hurt me the most was the rejection. I had been unable to understand why Andrew could not see me as the amazing person I was, how he could forget me being his 'Holy Grail.' When I comprehended that this had been all about him and not about me, it helped! I was finally healing!

Eventually, I was doing much better. I would wake up feeling peaceful and happy again. I was finally coming to grips with the drastic changes in my life. I was even using my gifts again, and my angel cards kept telling me that romance was heading my way. Within the next few weeks even! This absolutely thrilled me!

I decided that it was time to get ready to open another door by firmly closing an old one. I had done my very best. Maybe my relationship with Andrew was never meant to last. But, it had prepared me for a happy, lasting partnership with someone else by allowing me to work through my issues in a safe environment. For that, I would always be grateful to him.

It took some courage to let go of the familiar and to choose the unfamiliar, the unknown. In the past, fear had kept me from taking this step, but I finally found the courage within me. I wished Andrew well and much happiness but decided that I would no longer be open to us getting back together. I was done with the push-pull game we had been playing for too long.

One last time, I allowed the pain of possibilities lost to flow through me, the tears to fall, and the grief to surface. I stayed with those emotions, observed them without judgment, truly felt them without shrinking from them, and, just as the book "The 10 Second Miracle' had promised, felt them dissolve.

It was incredible! Just by allowing those feelings, I had taken their power! From then on, I felt better every day. I was almost back to my old, happy self. I started to laugh more, dance again, and sing along with my favorite songs.

Life was beautiful once again, and I felt free for the first time in a very long time.

⋆¸⸜⸝¸⋆

After that breakthrough, my creativity was on the rise as well. I was back to editing the sequel to my latest publication. Then, out of the blue, one of my vivid dreams led to another project. I loved it! A new tale to explore and occupy my time! Where would it lead? What twists and turns would find their way into the book? Only time would tell, but I was busily writing once more.

The dream had been even more vivid and real than my usual ones! And, the emotions I had felt had been extremely intense. I had been absolutely fascinated by the idea of loving a man who could shift forms between human and animal.

What would it be like to have such an incredible gift? To be able to explore the world from a whole new perspective? I wondered what this dream was trying to tell me. Could it be that there was more to my future mate than I had anticipated?

I remembered very clearly that I found this man absolutely gorgeous in both shapes. I could distinctly recall his clothes. He had worn a white, loose shirt, dark britches, and black boots. Kind of old fashioned but perfectly suited for him.

But, try as I might, I could not recall his face. Whenever I tried to concentrate on it, all I managed to remember was a sense of well-shaped features, but they were always blurred. To say that I found this annoying is putting it mildly!

⋆¸⸜⸝¸⋆

In the dream, we had locked eyes as he had slowly turned into a huge wolf right there in front of me. Once he had completed the change, he had made his way towards me. His mesmerizing gaze had never left mine and had held me in place. I had felt no fear. Once he was right there in front of me, without a second thought or a moment's hesitation, I had wrapped my arms around his thick neck.

I had buried my face in his soft fur and had inhaled the slightly musky scent of my new friend. He had smelled of trees, and moss, and wild chases through woods and meadows, of sunshine and moonlight. Just being close to him had given me such comfort, and some more bits of my pain over losing Andrew had drifted away. All of a sudden, I was almost whole again! Most of the remnants of that deep ache in my heart were gone!

I had smiled happily and then stepped back just enough so that I could see his face. The wolf's and my eyes had connected again as if drawn by some inexplicable magic. This was truly a large animal, but I had not an ounce of apprehension. I had known instinctively that he would never harm me, that if anything, he was my protector.

A funny thing had happened next. When I had moved back, I had maintained physical contact between us. My left hand had remained resting on one giant shoulder. A sudden movement had drawn my attention, and as I watched curiously, a strand of my new friend's hair had detached itself.

Right there, in front of my very eyes, it had begun to braid itself into a band which then had wrapped itself around the ring finger of my left hand!

I had raised the hand to my face so that I could regard the object up close. It was definitely a ring, intricately woven, and quite beautiful to behold. I had been delighted and had smiled with pleasure at having received such a special gift.

"Thank you," I had whispered. Speaking out loud had just felt wrong, as if it would have broken the spell of what was happening between us.

The wolf had stepped closer and placed his forehead against mine. I had heard a distinct voice in my mind, 'With your permission, I claim you as mine.' It had said gently.

'May my magic protect you and bring you to me soon, my love.'

At that point, I had woken up. I had been amazed. My entire being had been filled with a sense of total well-being. I had not felt so happy and peaceful in a long time. Holding up my left hand in front of my face, I had checked my ring finger. I had been stunned.

I remember thinking, 'Is it my imagination, or is there a faint outline of a band? Now, this is weird! Was this more than just a mere dream?' The longer I had looked at the faint mark, the more I had been filled with a sense of intense wonder.

✦⋆⋆

Everything changed from that night on. I was suddenly over the breakup. I was once again filled with boundless joy and so very content. I was even able to fend off Andrew's attempt to change my mind about moving on. To my surprise, I felt nothing but compassion for him when he suddenly showed up on my doorstep. It was as if my heart had been claimed by another.

My ex even brought beautiful roses; store-bought! This was something he had never done in all the years we had been together. He told me that he missed and loved me, that I had been right all along, that I was the one woman for him, his best friend, and that he was prepared to work together to make things work. Andrew was even willing to make a full commitment to our relationship, right then and there!

At one time, hearing this would have made me the happiest woman alive. All the words he spoke, I had so longed to hear just a few weeks ago. Now, they just filled me with sadness for him. He had waited too long!

I looked at him and told him with deep empathy and as kindly as possible that it was too late and that I believed that we were better off apart. What I did not share with him was that all the magnetism I had once felt for him was gone. I could not understand that myself, I had always seen him as very attractive. Wishing him well, I sent him on his way.

That evening, my brother and I went out to dinner to celebrate. He was incredibly proud of me for standing my ground. To be honest, I was pretty pleased with myself. I had finally done it! I had set myself free, opened the door to new possibilities, and embraced that I deserved a better tomorrow!

⁘

After that, my creativity soared to all new heights. My latest story seemed to just flow out of me like a dam had been broken. If I kept going like that, I would have the book published within three months! That was a record for me. It usually took me about a year to write and edit one of my tales. Not having all that negative energy of an up and down relationship hanging over my head seemed to do wonders for my art as well as my wellbeing!

I even started dating! A call out of the blue led to one of the most fun dates I had ever had. More dates with several different men followed. Wherever I went, even at the store or at the park, I got asked out. If my instincts said yes, I accepted.

Since I was choosing carefully, I enjoyed my outings with each and every one of these guys tremendously. But, after getting to know them a bit, none of them felt quite right. They were just not him!

My friends kept remarking how strange it was that I seemed to all of a sudden magically attract men. I could only agree. When my girlfriends and I went out to lunch, we came home with phone numbers, if we went to a bar or a dance, we were quickly surrounded by interested fellows. I was not the only one to benefit from that.

⁘

Each and every one of the guys I did go out with mentioned the intense draw they had felt towards me. It was all very puzzling, but I took it as a welcome gift and now had plenty of hiking, kayaking, and even sailing buddies. Life was a true pleasure, full of fun and adventures.

The writing was flowing at an incredible rate, I had good company available to me anytime I wanted it, and anything that had given me a bit of a problem in the past seemed to magically smooth itself out. I had come to appreciate that I was leading an even more charmed existence than ever before.

Spring turned into early summer. My latest story had been published in record time and was doing amazing. The Universe definitely had a hand in that one! I was now working on the next one. Even though, I was still single, I had never been more content and happier. All of my books were doing great, and I was genuinely enjoying myself.

Part of me was still longing for an intimate connection with that special someone, but I no longer felt overwhelmed, lost and alone. Ever since that incredible dream, something inside me had shifted.

I knew, could just feel it in my gut, in my very bones, that somehow, someday, I would meet that one man destined to walk beside me. Then, I would experience the amazing love I kept writing about. Mutual love, respect, admiration, and appreciation, as well as best friend chemistry, and great sexual chemistry, were well worth waiting for as far as I was concerned.

A great source of comfort and happiness for me was the frequent presence I sensed around me since the night I met the wolfman. It felt as if my true love's spirit was already with me, was already part of my life.

I was sure that soon he would join me in person, but for now, I was good!

Chapter 1

An Unexpected Invitation

While having lunch one day, my brother and I got the idea to vacation together. It was a spur of the moment decision, and we were afraid that it would be hard finding lodgings at such a late date. After all, July was rapidly approaching. Most places in the San Juan Islands were booked out months in advance, and we were now only two weeks out.

This time of year, business would be just a little slower for Richard, and he could take a week off without upsetting his clients. Having had this fabulous notion at such a late date, we were now hustling to find a place to go. We were looking for a nice hotel, somewhere quiet. We both loved the San Juans, but most accommodations were either already completely filled up or too busy to suit our taste.

Just as we had discarded yet another location, we each received a fancy, tastefully embossed envelope in the mail. The ornate lettering was printed in raised gold script, and a magnificent crest had been placed above the name and address. It was beautifully done, very classy, but kind of old fashioned. At first glance, my impression was that it came from a really luxurious and exclusive resort.

We were looking for a quiet, out of the way place, and this envelope most certainly did not give that kind of an impression. It screamed expensive and could have a bunch of rather wealthy people in attendance, not necessarily what we had in mind. We wanted to get away from it all.

✦✦✦

I had just about tossed the envelope into the garbage unopened, but, at the last moment, something stilled my hand. Almost against my will, I broke the seal. Only then did I realize that this was an actual wax seal! That alone was stunning. I had no idea that anyone used those anymore!

The paper of the letter inside was equally as expensive as its cover, and I unfolded it carefully. A colored catalog fell out and onto the table. The last time I had seen anything even close to this in attention to detail and quality had been in Europe. This definitely had a continental air to it!

To my immense pleasure, it was an invitation. Was I glad that I had not thrown it away! My brother and I would be able to stay at this exclusive resort for free the first week, and the second week was being offered at a truly minimal price! Not that money was a problem for either one of us, but this was beyond tempting!

An additional bonus and draw for both of us was the assurance that there would be few other guests. Now that was amazing! How could any place in the islands afford to not be totally booked out in July? Summers here in the Pacific Northwest are not that long, and the main tourist season here is in July and August!

✦✦✦

On some level, I was really not that surprised. All kinds of unanticipated windfalls had been coming my way of late.

My friends had noticed this and frequently commented on all the blessings flowing into my life.

Therefore, I brushed this startling invitation off as just another incident brought about by the amazing luck I seemed to have of late. I had no clue that much more was at play here!

After a brief discussion, Richard and I decided to accept the more than generous offer. We rearranged our busy schedules to take advantage of this unexpected opportunity. To us, it seemed to be fate that the perfect place had come along at just the right time.

⸎

The pictures in the catalog showed a very exclusive hotel in a truly magical setting. It was called 'The Haven' and promised great hiking in a secluded area, as well as the prospect of a variety of watersports. Just what we needed!

We were both curious about the resort and were looking forward to our well-deserved vacation. It had been years since my brother and I had been on holiday together. We both saw this upcoming time as an excellent chance to renew our friendship and love for each other.

Life had been so busy, and it would be fun to catch up. We had not managed to spend any great amount of time together for a couple of months now. The last time we had seen each other on an almost weekly basis had been during the period I was grieving for Andrew.

⸎

The resort we had been invited to was off the beaten track, on a private island only approachable by boat. As exclusive as it was, it lacked some of today's amenities such as cellphone reception and internet.

This was actually not a problem for us since we had both been working hard and needed a break. Therefore, Richard and I felt that we could survive quite well for a couple of weeks without our devices. The hotel did have a landline for emergencies, and that was all we needed.

The area around the resort was perfect for hiking, kayaking, sailing, and even bicycling. Most of the island was wooded, and it sported a number of trails, anything from easy walking to challenging climbs. We would have to work our way up to those, but this was a fabulous opportunity to advance my 'getting more fit' agenda.

The closer the time got to our departure, the more my excitement grew. I had packed and unpacked several times already and had finally gone out and bought a few additional classy, floor-length outfits that would stand up to any formal occasion.

The resort was rather fancy in its own unique way. It was medieval or Renaissance theme-based, and this was a welcome excuse to acquire a few extra costumes. After all, an author can never have enough props!

Naturally, I would be taking my computer. I can write anywhere, no internet required. The editing of the sequel was coming progressing nicely, and just a few minutes a day would get me further along. No matter where I was or what I was doing, working on my books just added that extra little bit of happiness to my days.

※※※

I was a bit anxious, however, about leaving my pets. My house sitter and friend always had them well under control, but I am used to their company, and I would miss them. And, they would most certainly miss me. But, John tended to spoil them rotten, and they loved him. I felt truly blessed to have him as my friend.

Richard and I had debated about taking the little guy along since Micha was a trained service dog. After some discussion of the pros and cons, we had decided that my German Shepherd would be terribly lonely without him.

Arianna adored John but would do much better with her little friend present. The two were usually inseparable, even if they did argue on occasions. It was either taking both with us or leaving them home.

※※※

Finally, the day of our departure was almost here. The morning before, I got ready to head to Richard's house in the city. I left around 1 PM, hoping to avoid the worst of the traffic. To my surprise, I ended up making really good time, a miracle in the Seattle area!

My brother and I had agreed that it would be wise for me to spend the night at his place. It was much closer from North Seattle to Anacortes than from my home on the Key Peninsula. As an additional bonus, I would be avoiding the morning rush hour.

My car would remain at my brother's house while we were gone. There was no sense in driving up there separately; not only a waste of gas, but it would have also deprived us of each other's company. And, I would not have to wake up quite as early to get on the way to meet up with the private ferry to the island.

We found out, however, that the service the resort was willing to offer went beyond what we had expected. We had intended to take Richard's vehicle, but that evening we received a surprising phone call from the manager of the hotel.

The man introduced himself as Alexander. After telling us how much they looked forward to having us as guests and inquiring if we had any other special requirements beyond our dietary ones, the manager enlightened us that a car would arrive at 9AM to pick us up. When I voiced my astonishment, the administrator politely pointed out that it was all in the welcome package.

After hanging up the phone, Richard and I looked at each other in complete wonder. Then, we went rushing to dig out our letters. Sure enough, there it was, in the catalog! Part of the package was a chauffeur. How could we have missed this? We had been over this brochure from cover to cover!

Something told me that there was no way we would have overlooked such an important detail, especially since it was right there in plain sight. Both Richard and I have close to photographic memories. I was almost certain that this little fact had not been there before.

How was that possible? New words could not suddenly appear in a brochure, or could they?

Chapter 2

On the Way

The next morning, just as promised, a car arrived to pick us up. The chauffeur politely introduced himself as Carlo. He was exceedingly courteous and went out of his way to make my brother and me as comfortable as possible. This must be what it felt like to be royalty! Well, I, for one, could get used to this!

The drive to Anacortes was pleasant and went by much faster than we had expected. A well-maintained ferry was waiting for us at the dock, and soon we were on our way. I was naturally on deck taking pictures. The incredible beauty of the San Juans never fails to enthrall me, and I love harbor towns like Anacortes.

Every time I visited; I fell deeper in love with the area. It spoke to me, called to me. Watching the islands passing by felt like coming home. The thought occurred to me, not for the first time, that maybe I should move there. The San Juans were most certainly very tempting to me.

I had been considering relocating for a while now. Only my friends and the fact that I genuinely loved my house had kept me from exploring this option more seriously.

⤜✦⤛

The staff of the boat was very attentive and really friendly. At 1 PM, Richard and I were served a fabulous meal. I was thrilled and impressed with the care that had been taken in the selection as well as the preparation. The resort had remembered that I needed gluten-free options and that my brother had various dietary requirements due to his past illness.

A table had been set up on the upper deck to give us the best view. In spite of being out there on the water, on a ferry no less, this was one of the most fabulous meals I have ever had. Not only was the food amazing, but the landscape passing by was magical. How much I loved this place and how much I had missed it!

In the years we were together, Andrew and I had sailed these islands extensively. He could be attentive, kind, and just plain amazing. Those days and our adventures together will be memories I will treasure forever.

I have no idea whatever happened to us or when we became so displeased with each other. But, that was in the past, and I resolutely pushed the memory away.

⤜✦⤛

The further we traveled towards our destination, the more my conviction grew that I needed to find a house in the area. Yes, winters would be harder than at my present home. It could get very cold and windy out here, but summers were just plain magical. Also, the deep feeling of connection I experienced whenever I was in the San Juan Islands would make it worth it.

The deep blue sky contrasted by the dark green trees, the variety in vegetation, shape, and sizes of these magnificent islands, and the sun sparkling on the dancing water of the Puget Sound always made me fall in love with this place over and over again and more so each time.

The pull to remain, to live out here, and to just create my own little world far away from everything I had known became almost overwhelming the longer we traveled.

⚜

After several hours of weaving our way through the San Juans, our destination finally came into sight. The island was beautiful in every way. The tall, dark trees; the sheer rock faces of high cliffs; the gentle green of small meadows, some leading down to sheltered bays; the bright sunshine; and the calm water around us created a truly enchanting setting.

I made my way up to the bridge so that I could see better. I did not want to miss a thing, and from up here, I had the best view of this tranquil piece of land which was to be our home for the next couple of weeks. The crew of the boat was very accommodating, and nobody objected to my presence in their space.

At the far end of the island, towards the west, I could make out some structures that must belong to the resort. The buildings seemed to be all grouped together. As we got closer, I spotted a second area of structures. When I asked the captain, he told me that these were the houses of the other residents.

I found it interesting that the homes had been built in clusters, just like most European habitations. I had also noted that the crew was very smartly dressed, very polite, and somehow different from the other workers of ferry boats I had seen.

I decided that this data was something to file away for the moment. I would exam my observations at leisure once I had more information. Maybe then I could make sense of it all.

⚜

The chauffeur politely helped us back into the car once we were securely docked. Richard and I assumed that Carlo would drive us straight to our accommodations, but to our surprise, we headed towards a large building close to the small harbor.

To my delight, a horse-drawn carriage was waiting for us. Carlo transferred our luggage to this new vehicle and then helped us get comfortable on the richly upholstered bench. After my brother and I were settled, the chauffer hoped onto the coachman's seat and expertly guided the horses up the hill towards the interior of the island.

Before long, several signs pointing in different directions came into view. One was aimed towards the bunch of buildings, another towards the cluster of homes, yet another towards a small bay at the far side of the islands, and one back the way we had just come.

The one directing us to the hotel read, 'Wolf Haven Resort.' Wait a minute! I could have sworn that the catalog had called the place simply 'The Haven' when we had looked at it before! What was going on here?

I immediately dug out my catalog, and sure enough, it now said, "Wolf Haven!" Ok, one such thing I might have chalked up to having missed something but two? No way! My memory was excellent, and I had extensively perused this brochure.

There was definitely something out of the ordinary happening here, and I could not wait to find out more!

Chapter 3

A Very Mysterious Place

My first view of the hotel complex left me in total awe. Wolf Haven Resort turned out to be far more magnificent than the catalog had promised. The main building looked just like a fancy European mansion, much like the ones you see in the paintings of the Old English Masters!

White stone walls offset by dark wood beams, a red tile roof, ivy growing up the walls, and all the buildings had gargoyles. The place even had a stable, and I could see a number of horses in a nearby pasture.

There was not a car in sight nor any modern conveniences such as satellite dishes and such. The entire setup truly conveyed the feeling of having stepped back in time.

I was immediately captivated by these stunning dwellings and so busy taking pictures, I would have fallen over the stairs had Richard not steadied me. The brochure had not done this resort justice at all! It was far more grand and more intriguing than I could have imagined.

⟡

My senses finally tingled strong enough to get my attention. I suddenly realized that there was more to this place than met the eye. An air of mystique hung over the entire complex. What exactly had triggered my instincts I was unable to define at that moment, but I intended to find out.

Since the fantasy worlds of my books play in these kinds of settings, I was instantly completely intrigued. This resort would have fit right in one of my tales!

This place had a grandeur, an elegance about it that also reminded me of some of the old mansions in the Black Forest of Germany or of the Scottish Highlands! I had stayed in a castle before, but this hotel was far more magnificent and attractive to me.

I wondered what the rest of the island was like. Had the appearance of being in the middle ages, someplace truly magical where a unicorn might saunter around a corner at any moment, been maintained everywhere? I was really looking forward to exploring it in detail.

I could not believe that we were so fortunate to have been invited to stay here for the next two weeks!

⟡

As it turned out, my brother and I shared an entire suite. Our bedrooms were separated by a large living area tastefully decorated with a leather couch, a black marble coffee table, and several comfortable chairs. A small kitchen allowed for some cooking and the fridge was already stocked with items both Richard and I enjoyed. This place was almost too good to be true!

We each had our own bathroom right off the bedroom. Mine was an absolute dream! Black granite floors offset by pure white marble walls and a bathtub which looked like it had been hewn out of one single huge block of quartz crystal! I had never seen anything like it! To top it all off, it even had jets and a comfortable headrest.

All kinds of fancy glass bottles of soaps, shampoos, conditioners, and such were available for my pleasure on a small shelf within easy reach. A skylight directly over the tub would allow me to see the moon as I leisurely soaked. This was just plain heaven!

The furniture in the suite alone must have cost a fortune! Most of it looked antique and was made of real wood, not cheap particle board. The air of the entire mansion exuded class and old money. Most of it was completely true to an era long passed, only a few modern conveniences such as electricity had been allowed.

How right up my alley since the times of the knights and ladies, of kings and queens, heroes and villains were the favorite settings for my books! Maybe that era drew me because I enjoyed a code of honor, valor, and gallantry in men?

This extraordinary place would most certainly give wings to my imagination. I was so glad that I had brought my computer. My brother had voiced his objections but had relented in the end. Separating me from my bliss is just about impossible when I am working on a book!

⁘⁘⁘

Dinner that night was a real treat. To our surprise, we were the only guests in the formal dining room. The staff was all magnificently attired in elaborate historical outfits. Good thing that I had just invested in some additional suitable clothes. I would need them!

When we had entered the lobby for the first time, it had truly been like stepping back in time. To my absolute delight, we had discovered that all the staff at the resort wore period costumes. I had stopped and gawked at all the splendor and attention to detail. I had not been able to help myself. No expense had been spared to portray utter realism of ages long past.

This was so perfect! It was like living one of my fantasies! All kinds of ideas started to instantly flood my brain, and while my brother checked us in, I was making notes of all those notions flowing into my mind.

This hotel had such sophistication, such class, such stunning beauty! I absolutely loved it! For some reason, I felt more at home here almost immediately than I had ever felt in any strange place.

The maître d' had noticed my rapt attention. After dealing with the registration, the attractive, tall, slender man had come over to where I was sitting busily writing and had introduced himself. His name was Allan.

Having observed my interest in the costumes, he had pointed out a small boutique tucked away in a corner of the lobby of the grand hotel. One quick glance had told me everything I had needed to know. After dropping my bags off in my room, I had immediately returned to the shop.

Half an hour later, I had returned to my room with a young man in tow. The poor guy was laden down with my latest acquisitions. All the costumes I had acquired were of amazing quality, and the extremely low prices had stunned me! The stitching was superb, the material soft and subtle, the colors deep and vibrant.

Every one of these outfits would be perfect for one of my book covers! Not only had I bought some beautiful clothes which pleased me immensely, but they were even a tax write-off!

Since we intended to explore the island in the morning, Richard and I decided to go to bed early. I could, however, not resist the allure of that amazing tub. After saying goodnight to my brother, I ran myself a hot bath.

To create an even more tranquil atmosphere, I lit the candles scattered throughout the room. Before long, I was soaking in the steaming water.

To make things even more perfect, the beautiful music of Celtic Woman, one of my favorite groups, was playing softly in the background. The magnificent setting, the enchanting music, the warmth cradling my body soon had me so relaxed that I must have fallen asleep.

'Wake up! Wake up, or you are going to drown in that tub! Woman, don't make me have to come up there to rescue you!' a voice shouted in my mind. Disoriented, I shook my head and sat up, sputtering. I had indeed been about to slip under the water!

⚘

Had it not been for that rather loud shout in my mind, I may have drowned. I seemed to have been tired enough! Who was this man who had been in such a panic at the inadvertent danger I had found myself in? Somehow I thought that his voice had sounded familiar, but I was too sleepy to try to figure all this out at that moment.

Then it came to me, and it hit me like lightning! I had been dreaming of him again, the man who turns into a wolf! We had been walking together somewhere in the woods. Maybe even on this island. We had been holding hands and had been in deep conversation until he had stopped and pulled me towards him.

I could still almost feel the passionate kiss that had followed. My lips seemed to be tingling. What must it be like to be kissed with such sweetness, such love, such ardor in real life?

Too bad that magical moment had been so rudely interrupted by my sliding too low in the water!

⚘

Sleepily, I fell into my bed and was soon dreaming of him again. Once more, I found myself in his arms. The feeling of familiarity, of being safe and protected, of coming home was so intense that it woke me up out of a deep slumber.

My heart ached with a longing I had never known before. That startling feeling was so strong that tears started rolling down my face, and I could not hold back a forlorn sob.

Being that upset, it took me a while to relax. So many thoughts were running through my mind. Who was that amazing man who I found myself so incredibly attracted to? Who had shouted to get my attention while I was in the tub?

Since I had no way of finding answers, I eased those churning emotions by giving them my undivided attention. I allowed myself to fully experience that terrible sense of loss and stayed with it as long as it took. Finally, the flow of chi was reestablished, and the yearning ebbed away.

As I cuddled further under the covers, I suddenly felt phantom arms slide around me. At first, I was stunned and maybe even a little afraid, but then a sense of being home and safe broke through my panic. This seemed very familiar!

I allowed myself to completely relax into the warmth of that loving embrace. Soon, I was sound asleep.

Chapter 4

Strange Events

When I awoke the next morning, I had a faint memory that something unusual had happened the night before. But, try as I might, I could not recall it. I discovered to my extreme astonishment that the water was still in the bathtub and that my towel was on the floor right outside the bathroom. Further adding to the puzzle was the fact that my pajamas were still laid out on the bed.

I must have been more tired than I had thought and just crawled under the covers. That was the only thing I could think of, but a faint niggling sensation kept worrying at me. My instincts told me that I was missing something and that it was important.

I can usually remember my dreams, but not this morning. I had a vague sense that a recollection of some significance was in my mind but just out of reach. It felt almost like I was being blocked from those elusive thoughts. Every time I tried to put my attention on them, it seemed to just slide off. Strange!

⋆⁘⋆⦵⋆⁘⋆

Since we intended to go hiking that day, I quickly got dressed and applied some minimal makeup. I felt peaceful and calm, but kind of out of it, almost like there was a veil between me and the rest of the world. This was a rather odd sensation I had no explanation for, but I assumed it would pass with some rigorous exercise.

Richard gave me an inquiring look when we met up in the living area of our suite. "Are you ok?" came his concerned question.

"I feel great, just a little off. Why? Do I look tired or something?" I asked him curiously.

"No, not exactly tired. There is just something different about you. I can't quite put my finger on it at the moment, but I am sure that it will come to me. Let's head down to eat!" With a gentlemanly bow, my brother opened the door for me, and the two of us headed for the beautiful wide staircase in the center of the mansion.

⋆⁘⋆⦵⋆⁘⋆

Breakfast was already laid out by the time we reached the dining room. I was thrilled at all the gluten-free options. The rotund cook came out and introduced himself. The delightful man, he told us that his name was George, had even gone through the trouble of baking fresh rolls for me! The smell and taste alone were amazing, and I asked if I could take a couple with me for our picnic on the hike.

Two cups of coffee later, and with enough food for a good-sized lunch in our backpacks, we were heading out the door. Richard and I had decided to wear long pants and boots since this made it possible for us to go off the trails as well. We also carried light jackets just in case.

I was almost bouncing with excitement, especially tanked up on caffeine. One cup was usually my limit. Add to this that I absolutely adore discovering new areas - I was

~ 28 ~

raring to go! In the bright sunshine, this place just invited investigation, and I could not wait to see it all!

⤞✤⤝

My brother and I spent the rest of the morning exploring the woods to the north of the resort. Around noon, we worked our way towards the water and looked for a pleasant spot with a view. We found the perfect place on top of a bluff overlooking a small bay. Here, we had our picnic. We were relaxed, happy, and enjoying our time together.

While we were having our delicious snacks, we were joined by a flock of small birds. After some initial hesitation, they started eating right out of my hand! I was absolutely delighted. Richard and I were both falling in love with this magical island.

The view from the spot we had chosen was magnificent. We could see other islands off in the distance as well as a grouping of rocks which reminded me of Nessie, the Loch Ness monster. The sunlight on the water was mesmerizing and lulled us into a tranquil state of utter peacefulness.

After we caught ourselves nearly falling asleep, we decided to pack up and move on. We wanted to explore just a little further this day and taking a nap right here on the mossy rocks was not on our agenda.

⤞✤⤝

For much of the rest of the afternoon, Richard and I worked our way east along the top of the cliffs high above the water. The sun lit up our surroundings and gave them that warm, pleasant feeling and smell of early summer. We were enjoying ourselves immensely.

When we came across a trail leading south a while later, we decided to take it. Richard and I assumed that it would lead us back towards the resort. All that hiking had made both of us hungry, and we were looking forward to dinner.

Within a few minutes of starting on this new path, I began to sense something odd. Where there had been warm and bright sunshine an instant ago, fog was now rolling in and thickening by the moment. Could this be coming in from the Sound? Since we did not want to get lost in the increasing whiteness, we sped up our pace in the hope to outpace the growing murkiness.

Before too much longer, it got harder and harder to stay on the trail. My brother and I were proceeding with ultimate caution. We were afraid of getting lost or backtracking towards the shore and the tall, steep cliffs.

Then, just after we had pushed our way through an especially dense bank of mist, we found ourselves near a circle of stones.

The unexpected discovery brought both Richard and me to a dead stop. We were stunned. This site was amazing, almost like a small Stonehenge! But, how had it gotten here?

Who had built it? It was definitely old and had been here for a very long time. We had heard of no such place in the San Juans!

As I stepped closer, drawn by deep curiosity and an unexplainable sense of needing to step within, I could feel the hum of magic from these ancient megaliths.

Richard grabbed me just as I was about to enter the circle. "I can sense something, there is some sort of power here. Let's not be hasty, little sister. Let's ask our host about this place first before we go blundering into who knows what. I know you love to explore, but I just have a feeling about this. Ok?"

His words jolted me awake from a near trance. The draw of the circle had been that intense. I could not deny the wisdom of Richard's words. There was definitely something strange going on here.

I felt a brief sense of regret, but Richard was right. There was no good reason to blunder into possible danger. I gave my brother a grateful look. Had it not been for him, I would have entered within.

After one last longing glance at the tempting enigma, I followed my sibling. We carefully circumvented the standing stones and picked the path back up on the other side.

Once again, the fog closed in around us. This time even thicker than before. Richard and I decided to hold hands to prevent losing each other. The visibility was so poor that my brother was using a stick to feel our way.

We continued to make slow but steady progress. Then, all of a sudden, we came out into brilliant sunshine. We could see the resort off in the distance.

When we looked back, the path we had just almost blindly walked along on, was perfectly clear! Now, this was truly weird!

⚬∿⚘⚘∿⚬

That evening, Richard asked our waiter, Jeffrey, about the stone circle we had happened upon. The man claimed no knowledge of such a place on the island, but a strange expression crossed his face.

Was it awe? Or was it fear? It could have been either or neither, I was not sure. But, of one thing, I was certain. This delightful isle definitely had its mysteries!

At that moment, it occurred to me that strange events may actually be the norm here. As soon as that thought entered my mind, I recalled the changes in the catalog as well as the events of the morning.

Finding the towel on the floor and the bath still full had definitely been out of character for me. The entire incident had been more than a little odd, especially since I had no recollection of how I had gotten into that bed. Nor of my dreams, for that matter.

Why did I keep having the feeling that something important was hidden behind the thick fog that stood between me and last night's memories?

Chapter 5

The Circle

The waiter's response had convinced me that there was more going on here on this lovely little island than we were supposed to know about. Later, I watched Jeffrey through the open doors to the lobby. He was talking in a very urgent manner to the maître d', Allan. Both kept glancing in our direction, so I was fairly certain that they were talking about Richard and me.

After a wonderful dinner, my brother and I decided to have a glass of wine. Since the evening was balmy and calm, we were delighted to be able to move out onto the west-facing patio to watch the sun go down.

That it remains light here so late in the summers is one of my absolute favorite things about the Pacific Northwest. To me, it never stops feeling magical to be out at almost 10PM and still be able to see. I genuinely miss those long evenings when fall comes around.

Slowly, the deep blue sky took on hues of orange and red, which then darkened to shades of purple. The trees became black shadows, and the islands in the distance gradually faded away in the twilight. What a stunning sunset! How lucky were we to have two weeks of such beauty!

This resort was truly magnificent, so tranquil and peaceful. And, so full of secrets! To say I was intrigued as well as already deeply in love with the place, as much or more than I was with the rest of the San Juans, is putting it mildly.

This was pure perfection. Not only gorgeous surroundings but also a hint of something otherworldly. I love a good mystery, and there was definitely something here worth looking into.

⚜

Since I am a medium, among other things, I am fairly good at picking up on the vibrations of places and people. I have very astute instincts and perceptions, gifts that I now treasure greatly. This was not always the case. As a child, being so sensitive to others' emotions often left me traumatized and confused. It took many years before I could fully embrace all that I am.

Since there was definitely something out of the ordinary going on here, I decided that maybe it was time to use my other senses to get some answers. But not here, out in public, where I could be observed. My gut told me that any psychic exploration had to be done from the safety of our rooms. As it was, the sun had completely set by now, and the remaining light was starting to dwindle.

"Shall we return to our rooms, Richard?" I asked my brother, setting down my empty glass. "I want to send out my senses and explore the island in that fashion. Would you please watch over me while I am doing this?"

Richard gave me a sharp look. He and I are very close, and he is almost as perceptive as I am. "Are you sure about that? What if you come across something that is beyond what you can handle? I am certain that there is more to this place than can be seen!"

"I don't feel that there is anything here that has the intent to hurt me, rather the opposite. Something was drawing me into that circle, and if the staff will not provide us with answers, I am determined to find them another way!" I reassured him.

"As long as you are certain, little sister! Shall we?" responded my amazing brother. He was always so supportive and truly a very remarkable man. Honest, understanding, empathetic, and kind. And no, I am not just saying that because he is my brother. Richard is a wonderful man.

Always a gentleman, my brother presented me with his arm. Waving goodnight to the staff, we headed up the grand stairs and to our suite.

~ ~ ~

After retrieving one of the candles from the bathroom and lighting it, I made myself comfortable on the couch in the living room. Then, I centered myself. Richard sat down in a chair next to me. He knew what to watch for and, if he felt that I was in any sort of trouble, he would shake me to bring me back into my body.

Taking several calming breaths, I shielded myself before allowing myself to slide into a deep trance. I began to push my mind outward, to expand first into the ether of the room then beyond. Soon I was sensing, feeling all that was around us.

Detecting no evidence of danger nor any kind of threat from any direction, I began to concentrate on specific areas that drew me. One of these was the circle of stones. In my mind's eye, I could see the translucent, shimmering aura of power surrounding each one of the rocks.

The colors washing over the megaliths ranged from pure white all the way to indigo and were continually changing! Arches of light connected the stones. What a fascinating and magnificent display! We will definitely have to explore the circle further, I decided right then and there.

I was too curious not to examine this phenomenon closer. Soon, I was happily playing in the auras and the lights of the ancient circle. I let the sparkling energy flowing around the stones wash over and through me, and it felt absolutely amazing! The sensation was like absorbing an entire pot of coffee all at once! I felt rejuvenated and vibrantly alive.

⁕⁂⁕

Suddenly, a person stepped within. I had noticed movement out of the corner of my eye and turned to face the intruder interrupting my fun. At the sight of him, recognition dawned, and I froze in the middle of my dance of pure joy.

It was him! The man who could turn into the wolf! With a sudden jolt, I remembered my dreams from last night. Now I understood why access from them had been blocked! I could not help but turn a deep shade of red.

What had started with the innocent dream of walking hand in hand in the woods, had progressed much further during the night. I now recalled him setting my blood on fire with his mere touch! His kisses had caused a longing and want inside of me that had become almost unbearable, his hands roaming over my body and mine over his had sired a desire, a passion, that had been beyond anything I had ever experienced before.

I had wanted him so badly and he me that we had almost lost control. Panting, we had finally pulled apart. We knew deep inside that the time was not yet right. As urgently as we had craved each other, we realized that we needed to wait. I was not sure I would be able to maintain that resolve if he touched me again like he had done that night!

⁕⁂⁕

Standing stock-still within the glowing circle of stones, I wearily eyed the object of my dream's burning desire. Was he real or some sort of a phantom? I had to know before I lost any more of my heart to this man! To get the answers I wanted, needed, I would have to keep some distance between us.

Even now, I could feel the attraction between us. There was an intense magnetism emanating from him that drew me like a moth to the flame. It took all my willpower to resist it. If I let him come near me or stepped towards him, I was certain that my body, even in spirit form, would react just as it had when he had touched me before in my dream.

"Don't come any closer!" I warned him. "I have some questions for you! For starters, I need to know who and what you are and what is happening to me!"

Even so he acknowledged my request with a nod; he seemed to have decided to completely ignore it. The looks he gave me instead burned with passion and longing. He appeared to be just as resolute to have his way as I was determined to have mine.

A sort of dance resulted from our refusal to give in to the other. Anytime he stepped in my direction, I moved to evade him. With his continued attempts to cover the space between us, we were now vigilantly circling each other inside the powerful stones like two warriors preparing to do battle.

"Don't even think about it until I get an explanation!" I hissed at him. He may be gorgeous, and all I wanted was to touch him, be in his arms, but I was resolved to stand my ground.

"Do you know how beautiful you are when you are fierce like that, my Lady?" The infuriating man enquired. He was smiling! Boy, did that fire up my ire! I wanted to wipe that grin right off his face! I would have loved to have one of my practice swords in hand about now! How dare he think that this was amusing!

It was taking everything I had to keep myself from throwing myself in his arms, and he was giving me compliments and smiling at me! In frustration and anger, I stomped my ethereal foot. How about some answers instead?

"Tell me what this is all about! I want to know right now who you are!" I demanded through clenched teeth. He liked me ferocious, well he had seen nothing yet!

My weakness around him was making me more than a little testy. Matter of fact, I was getting downright furious! Not ever again would I allow a man as much power over me as I had granted Andrew! The desire to hit this exasperating guy with something was growing by the second! Not that I would, but still!

I had loved my ex with all my heart, my soul, everything I was. Unfortunately, he had not seen that privilege as the gift that it was, the treasure he had within his reach. I had placed him above me, a mistake I would never repeat!

I was strong now, self-assured, and confident and determined to stand my ground against any man, even one as gorgeous as this one who set my pulse racing with a mere look.

⁂

Attraction and desire had been something I had not felt in a long time. None of the good-looking men I had met over the last few months had even ignited the slightest of sparks. No chemistry, not a bit! My body's needs seemed to have died right along with the last of my passion for Andrew. Until last night when they had come roaring to life with a vengeance!

My handsome opponent had finally stopped pursuing me and was now casually leaning up against one of the stones. Jeez, this guy just oozed sexiness! How dare one man be this gorgeous! The pull I felt towards him was incredibly strong. This was some magnetism! More powerful than anything I had experienced before!

I wanted this guy more than I had ever desired anyone in my life! That alone was enough to really tick me off! This was dangerous, as far as I was concerned! I was not about to allow myself to be swept off my feet and end up hurt once again! I was stronger than that now, and if he thought I would give in that easily; he was in for a surprise!

Determined to stand my ground, I was glaring at the stunning stranger from the safety of my own megalith. He, in turn, was regarding me calmly. Was he enjoying my discomfiture and irritation? The thought alone was enough to increase my ire, and fury was beginning to roll off me in waves.

⚜

The strikingly handsome man continued to study me steadily. He was no longer smiling but watched me with puzzlement and confusion as well as concern. I don't think either of us had realized until that very moment how deep the hurt in my heart and soul had truly gone and how resolved I was to protect myself from now on.

Finally, he held up his hands. "My lady, I give! I had not anticipated your reaction after the affections we have already shared. The last thing I wanted to do was upset you! Let me assure you that I will do you no harm!"

My dream lover kept his voice soft and soothing; he spoke to me like one would to a wild animal on the verge of preparing to flee. Had I really been that on edge? The realization hit me hard, and my anger ebbed away. When my new friend saw my stance relax ever so slightly, he smiled at me reassuringly and continued.

"I am Taren, and as you already know, I can shapeshift, mostly from man to wolf. But, I can manage other forms as well. I am real, I live on this island, and I have brought you here," he informed me. Brought me here? Now my interest was definitely peaked!

"Our hearts and souls were bonded when you showed no fear and touched me in that very first dream! That night, you became the keeper of my very essence, all that I am. I want to love you, cherish you, adore you, and spend my life with you! You are everything I have searched for," Taren explained calmly.

His words rang true in my heart. I had no doubt that he meant every last one. And, I could feel the growing connection between us. The last remnants of the need to protect myself from this amazing man faded away. Relief flooded my system, and I allowed myself to relax further.

"I promise you that you are safe with me, now and forever! I will do my very best to never hurt you, nor will I permit another to cause you injury ever again! You are most precious to me, and I will protect you with my life if need be! Of that, I give you my solemn word!" Taren assured me. He was regarding me with all seriousness. There was no playfulness in him any longer, he meant what he said.

I could feel the effect of such a grave vow uttered inside this circle of stones. That he was willing to speak the words, to commit to such an unbreakable oath reinforced by the powers of old, told me a lot about the sincerity of this amazing man.

I calmed down completely. I could feel that Taren was a kind, compassionate, and empathetic person and that he would do his best to make me feel sheltered and loved. Was that what I craved most in a man after Andrew? Someone who made me feel protected, who was willing to be my rock?

I was stunned by that realization. Yes, I was strong, competent, and perfectly able to look after myself but longed to not have to do so with my partner! I wanted to concentrate on living, on creating without the constant need to be on guard!

That my reaction to this gorgeous man had been one resembling a wary wild creature filled me with sadness. Yes, I had always seen myself as fey, but that had been unexpected. I still had healing to do, but I was sure that with Taren at my side, processing some of the leftovers of the past would be a breeze.

Taren's eyes were intensely studying the expression on my face. He seemed to be in tune enough with me already to have been able to follow along with my realization. My gaze never left his as he approached, and I allowed him to pull me close.

"Growth is a journey, my love, and so is healing the wounds inflicted upon us throughout our lives. We both have them, but working together, we can put all that behind us, build a lasting, happy relationship and thrive," he muttered into my ethereal hair.

I pulled back a little and smiled up at him. My heart felt much lighter all of a sudden. Sensing the shift in my mood, Taren asked playfully, "Now, were those enough explanations? Would you go say goodnight to your brother and then return here to me from the comfort of your own bed? Please?"

✦❀⋆❀✦

Upon hearing his request, I gave a small laugh. When I tried to come up with a retort, nothing emerged. My voice seemed to have abandoned me, and all I could do was nod. This had most certainly been an enlightening evening!

After the emotional storm which had raged on inside me, feeling those strong arms around me was such a comfort! I knew that the desire to stay with Taren was going to overwhelm me if I did not leave this very moment. The idea of having those sensual hands roaming all over me while Richard was sitting right next to me was more than a little disturbing!

I needed to return to my body, but first, I had to get myself under control! If I left this trance in the high state of arousal I currently found myself in, my perceptive brother would catch on in a second.

Regretfully, I stepped away from Taren. I missed the shelter of his arms, but I would return soon. Taking some deep breaths, I walked out of the circle and away from the object of my burning desire. He needed to be out of my sight if I was ever going to manage to dampen down these raging feelings inside me!

⊱✿⊰

Taking yet another deep breath, I opened my eyes. I was determined to return to the circle as quickly as possible but wanted to do so without triggering my brother's suspicions.

"Ah, there you are!" Richard greeted me. He smiled and looked at me, inquiringly. "So, what did you discover? Anything worth reconnoitering further?"

"There is definitely something going on with that circle! The stones have the most amazing auras, white with occasional soft bands in all colors of the rainbow. It was absolutely beautiful, and we should explore it further in person!"

I acted as if I was suppressing a yawn. "Wow, that must have taken more out of me than I thought! I am so tired all of a sudden! If you don't mind, I am heading to bed. I need to get some sleep. I will tell you more about what I found out tomorrow!"

Richard gave me a sharp look. "Are you sure you're ok?"

"Yes," I responded, smiling. "Just a little weary. That little exploration took more of my energy than I had expected!"

Getting up from the couch, I pinched out the candle and gave my brother a hug. Richard held me at arm's length for a moment, and enquiringly searched my face before gently kissing me on the forehead.

"Goodnight, little sister, and sleep well. I love you."

"Goodnight, Richard! I love you too. I see you in the morning. And do not worry! I promise, I am just fine!" I replied as I disengaged myself and headed for my bedroom.

At the door, I turned and gave my brother a wave. I was surprised to see that Richard was still standing where I had left him. I noted the thoughtful expression on his face as I closed the door. I guess I had not managed to put him completely at ease.

✵

Had he caught on? Did he know that I was up to something? And exactly what was I getting myself into? Did I really want to return to that mesmerizing man in the stone circle? My heart, body, and soul most certainly did, but part of me remained just a tiny bit cautious. Could it hurt to go back and talk to him some more?

I would be in spirit form only, but that carried with it dangers all of its own. Energy attachments and such can be a real risk and the reason I always shielded myself. Not that it had done me all that much good within the influence of that magical circle!

The power of the ancient megaliths was such that I had been laid bare, had been dependent on its protection instead of my own. I had, however, even knowing this, felt totally at ease while dancing to the inaudible song of the Universe that had washed through me inside the circle. And, I was certain by now that Taren meant me no harm. In my estimation, it was safe to go back.

✵

Part of me wanted to rush back out and tell my brother the truth, but an even bigger part of me was drawn back to Taren. I hurried through my evening routine. Suddenly, I could not wait to return!

Just the thought of that gorgeous man made my stomach flutter, and my pulse begin to race. This guy was definitely dangerous to me. I knew that if I let him in my heart, he could hurt me even more than my breakup with Andrew had done.

Going back was taking a chance, a big one at that. Was I brave enough to let myself love again? But, how could I not? Was that not what I had always longed for? A happy, lasting relationship with a man who loved me as much as I loved him?

Could I deny myself the real possibility of such an amazing love because I was afraid? I was stronger than that! My decision was made.

Chapter 6

Dream Lover

As soon as I was done brushing my teeth, washing my face, and putting on cream, I hurried into the bedroom. Just as quickly as I could, I donned my pajamas and slid into bed. Pulling up the covers, I tried to get comfortable and to relax. I was, however, so excited at the prospect of my upcoming meeting with Taren that I was suddenly wide awake. This would not do!

Giving up trying to force myself into sleep, I decided to return into a trance. I realized that this was not all that safe here in this magical place alone in the bedroom, but some part of me knew that Taren would never allow anything nor anyone to hurt me. Funny how much trust I had in this stranger I had just met!

Taking deep breaths, I centered myself, shielded, and then sent my senses outward. Immediately, I was drawn in the direction of the circle. I streaked like lightning towards it.

Since it had taken so long to be on my way, part of me feared that Taren might have grown tired of waiting for me. But, there he was, sitting with his back against one of the megaliths, resting with his eyes closed. I allowed myself to drink in the stunning sight of him for a few moments. It was definitely not fair for a man to be so very gorgeous!

"Taren," I said softly, taking some hesitant steps towards him. With the agility of a cat, the incredibly handsome man rose to his feet. Did he have to be so darned sexy? So very appealing? How could any woman possibly keep her head around him?

"There you are, my love! You came! I was starting to think that I had scared you away!" he exclaimed. With just a few graceful steps, he covered the distance between us. I could feel the heat rising in my body with every inch he came closer to me!

"Stop! Stop right there!" I demanded, backing up. I needed just a few more answers before I allowed things between us to proceed. "What is it you want with me? What are your intentions towards me?"

As the words came out of my mouth, I became aware of how old fashioned they sounded. I felt kind of silly for a moment but then realized that those words conveyed precisely what I desired to know. Just what was he offering me? What did he want?

~ ❦ ~

Taren had stopped just inches from me. He was way to close already for comfort, and my heart was suddenly beating much faster. That man had the most devastating effect on me, but at least there was a tiny bit of distance between us. Not much, mind you, but just enough to hold onto some of my senses.

I was eying him warily. No man had the right to be this good looking! His kind, clear eyes were fringed by long dark lashes, his mouth was full and sensuous, just made for kissing. Against my will, my eyes focused on those tempting lips, and I had to tear my gaze away or risk losing my composure completely.

Taren's entire face was almost perfectly proportioned with a firm chin and chiseled cheekbones. He may not have been every woman's dream, but to me, he was beyond compare. Drop-dead gorgeous kept coming to mind as I was standing there, ogling him like a schoolgirl in love!

He was tall, with a built that promised an enticing body under that lose shirt. I seriously doubted that there was an ounce of fat on that well-muscled frame! His dark hair was wavy, parted at the side, and a lock of it had the tendency to fall onto his forehead. I don't think I could have imagined a better-looking man if I had tried!

But, for a long time, I had felt that way about Andrew. I had seen him as beautiful, inside and out. It was just his attitude towards our relationship that I had a problem with, not his looks or his soul. I had wanted a life with him so very much!

The Universe, however, had other plans for us. For the first time, I was genuinely good with that. Had fear not gotten the better of us, Andrew and I might still be together, and I would have missed out on meeting this fascinating and more than worthy man in front of me!

Was I already in love with Taren? There certainly was an almost irresistible draw towards him. The desire to touch him was so strong that I could barely resist it! Yes, the seeds had been planted, and it was time to permit them to grow!

⁂

Taren had watched me intently. He had not missed my eyes roaming over his face and body nor my thoughtful expression. "Do you like what you see?" he finally asked me with a smile.

"Yes," slipped out before I could help myself. My hand flew to my mouth. I could not believe that I had just said that! Had I not been in my spirit body, I am sure I would have turned beet red! But then, squaring my shoulders, I confidently returned his gaze. I vowed at that moment to always speak my mind and heart to this beautiful man.

"Thank you! It makes me happy that you feel that way! And I love your honesty! You are authentic, real! Do you know how charming you are? To me, you are so very irresistible!" he answered with an affectionate smile.

I looked at him with a stunned expression on my face. This vision of a man was almost too good to believe, and he knew just what to say! How much I had longed to hear these same words from a man I actually felt an attraction for! "You find me irresistible?" I asked in wonder.

"Yes, totally and completely so! You are the kind of woman I have been searching for for so long. You are beautiful inside and out, my Ella! Don't you know how special you are?"

I loved people but had always felt like I operated in a world set apart, a world filled with the coming alive of fantasy and endless possibilities. I just could not accept the limitations others seemed to perceive.

As a teenager, not being like others had bothered me. The resulting rejection had hurt, but I had made a conscious choice long ago that it was alright for me to be different, to live with my heart wide open. If this meant I was easier to hurt, so be it!

It was important to me to speak my truth. Since I had never wanted to hurt anyone's feelings, that had been difficult for me for a long time. But, since I learned to do it from a place of love, I can do it. Also, I try to help people and to be kind. Maybe that did make me special. It sure seemed to do so in Taren's eyes.

"Back to your questions, my beautiful lady. What I want with you is to love you like you have never been loved before. I have nothing but honorable intentions towards you and hope to make you my wife someday soon. Does this meet with your approval?"

This was the answer I had hoped to hear but not yet expected. My heart started to sing with pure joy. Taren was willing to give me the one thing that had been missing from my life for all those years! Love returned in equal measure! But, I had learned from the past and was no longer so easily swayed.

"How can you know that you want to marry me? We barely know each other!" I managed to squeeze out. The complete and utter honesty of his answer had taken me by surprise.

✵

The mention of marriage right off the bat had been somewhat unexpected. All this was moving just a little bit fast for my taste, but Taren struck me as a man who was self-aware enough to know what he wanted when he saw it. I admired his courage to come straight out and state his intentions.

This was not the first time that a man had wanted to marry me shortly after we met. But, never had one been as appealing as this one, nor had I ever seriously considered their offers like I was at this moment!

✵

Taren could have any woman he wanted. I had no doubt about that. With his good looks, who would be able to resist him? Not many, that was for sure. Would he accept that I did not share my man with another?

"What kind of a relationship do you have in mind? I mean, you are one of the most attractive men I have ever seen. There have to be many women available to you. Will one be enough for you?" I enquired regarding him through narrowed eyes.

Much depended on his answer. It was better to find out now where I stood than later. If I had to share this man, it would break my heart. I would rather walk away right this very minute than set myself up for that kind of pain!

I knew I could fall in love with Taren so deeply, so completely that there would be no turning back. My instincts told me that with him, the healthy, happy, lasting relationship I had dreamed of was possible. He could become the mate I had always longed for, dreamed of, the man to claim all of me by returning my feelings in full. If he was willing to be all in, so was I!

Taren smiled at me gently. "Sweetheart, I am a shapeshifter. We bond with one mate, and we bond for life, a very long life I might add! You will never have to share me with any other woman, I can promise you that! Anything else?"

I eyed the gorgeous man in front of me longingly and with some sadness. "I am older than you by a fair bit! If you live as long as you say, I will be gone years before you! How can I tie you to me knowing that?"

"Once you agree to become my bond-mate, on the next full moon, you will be offered an elixir that will not only make you younger but also lengthened your life to match mine. We will have a very long, happy life together, my love, I can promise you that!"

With those words, Taren gently and carefully reached out a hand towards me. He must have feared that I would flee if he moved too quickly. I am not sure, maybe I would have, but his searching gaze held me mesmerized and in place.

When his long, slender fingers caressed my face, my eyes closed involuntary. The sensation of that gentle touch sent an ache straight through my heart. I knew that I could love this incredible man with every ounce of my being and with a passion and ferocity that would put any other love I had ever felt to shame.

Was I brave enough to proceed? Was stopping this still possible? Or was I lost already, and it was too late to flee?

⊱•☙❧•⊰

I was plain terrified. To allow another such power to hurt me was the scariest thing I have ever faced. I realized that with Taren, there would be no half measures. Love would be flowing both ways which would strengthen it to a level that I had always dreamed of but had also secretly feared.

There had been a time that I had loved Andrew so deeply that I would have done just about anything for him. It had taken a lot of courage to love that intensely, but what I had felt then would be nothing compared to what Taren and I would be sharing.

Looking up at this amazing man who was offering me the one thing I had been missing and wanting my entire life, I quietly voiced my feelings. "I am afraid, but I long for a connection with you."

Taren stepped forward and enclosed my spirit body in his embrace. I was surprised by how solid I suddenly felt. My head came to rest against his well-muscled chest. "Oh sweetheart, I know that you have been hurt! I swear to you, I will do my very best to never allow anyone to hurt you again in any way, shape, or form. You are safe with me; I promise you that!" he murmured into my hair.

⸙⸙⸙

Being held in his arms felt like coming home. I felt safe and loved. Tears of relief started to roll down my face. My stomach unknotted itself as the powerful fear I had experienced a moment ago relaxed its grip only to be replaced by an entirely different emotion.

Desire like I had never felt before raced through my body. I pulled back just enough to be able to see his face. As our eyes met, Taren's darkened with need and untold emotions. He closed them for one deep breath before opening them once again and allowing me to see the true depth of his passion and love.

Our gazes locked, and the feelings we read in each other's faces filled both of us with wonder. There was longing, desire, and the promise of an incredible love, the kind of love most of us will taste only in dreams. Without him uttering a word, I knew that he felt as grateful and blessed as I did!

That was the moment I decided to throw all caution to the wind. I wanted this, and I would allow it. Suddenly feeling incredibly happy, I smiled up at Taren.

"Yes, I accept the bond and will be your mate," I told him solemnly.

His entire face lit up, and I was instantly smitten even further by the crinkle at the corner of his eyes and the warmth and joy I read in those moonlit orbs.

⁘⁘⁘

Next thing I knew, that sensuous mouth came down to greet mine and the kiss we shared left me breathless and my semi-solid spirit form filled with yearning. Good thing that my body rested safely on my bed in my room, away from the watchful eyes of my brother! When Taren pulled back, we were both panting with desire.

"I want you more than you will ever know, but we will have to wait to make love. For one, we both need to be in our physical bodies, my beautiful lady. And two, our law dictates that you need to take the elixir first and that our bonds are sanctioned in a wedding ceremony before we can become truly one," Taren said with sincere regret.

"I will miss holding you in my arms every single minute until we are reunited on the night of the full moon," he told me, pulling me close for one last hug.

⁘⁘⁘

I had no idea what was happening but knew that I was not going to like what was about to come. To be parted just as I had found him!

"Enjoy the island and let it work its magic on you, my dearest love. Soon, we will meet in person, and you will remember our agreement and the love we have for each other. For now, I need you to forget all but your visit to the circle of stones in your trance earlier today."

I pulled back with tears in my eyes. Forget about him? How was that even possible? I hated the thought of not remembering these special moments we had shared!

"My love! I don't like this either, but see no other way! I will never be far away, but we need to wait just a little while longer! I am only human, and you so tempt me!" Taren whispered, pulling me close once more.

"I will be thinking of you every moment of every day, but we need to wait for the full moon! It is only a few nights away, on the ninth day of your stay! Then, I will meet you here, and we will seal our bond." he explained.

"I would not ask this of you if there were any other way, my love. The waxing of the moon and the magic of the island will prepare your body and soul for the ritual. From now on, your gluten-free food will have a special ingredient that will speed things along. Do you trust me?" he finally asked.

With him, there would be no holding back how and what I felt, ever, this I promised myself. Therefore, looking him straight in the face, I answered from my heart.

"I trust you fully and completely," I solemnly replied. I could see the effect my words had on Taren.

"My love! What have I done to deserve such a beautiful soul such as you? I am the luckiest man alive, and you will never regret placing your trust in me nor loving me! I cannot bear to be parted from you either! I know it is bending the rules, but look for me in your dreams!" he uttered before kissing me one last time.

⸙

We looked deeply into each other's eyes as he spoke the words imbued with his magic.

"Sleep deep, and dream of me, my love. Forget all but visiting the circle of stones until we meet again soon. Let my love live and grow in your heart." With a kiss to my forehead, and a gentle touch to my chest, right above my heart, Taren sealed the spell.

The circle faded away, and I came out of my trance in the shelter of my bed. I had just enough time to register that I had returned to my room before I fell deeply asleep and began to dream.

Even if my dream was harmless compared to the passion I had felt being held by this incredible man, a smile played on my features all night long, and my heart was overflowing with happiness and love.

Chapter 7

Pleasant Days

When I awoke the next morning, I had no memory of the time I had spent in the circle of stones with Taren. As he had warned me, our meetings and the agreement we had made had been completely forgotten. I could, however, recall my dreams of that night.

A smile stole over my face as I recollected the tall, dark stranger I had strolled the streets of Paris with hand in hand. We had some delightful adventures, and he showed me some fantastic places. Now there was a man!

He was at least 6 foot something, slender but well-muscled, and gorgeous, that much I remembered, but his face was just a little bit fuzzy. I had almost been able to make it out, but not quite. I had finally just given up and had enjoyed our moments together.

The feelings between us had been intense, but he had been a perfect gentleman. Much to my frustration, I must admit. It had been a long time since I had wanted to touch and be touched, and I was not a nun after all.

One look at those long, slender, powerful fingers had made me long for him to run them through my shoulder-length hair, wrap them around my waist, or just have them caress my cheek. He finally had, it must have been towards morning, just before he gently cupped my face.

After looking deep into my eyes, he had kissed me passionately. As he tore himself away, the longing I saw on his face had about broken my heart. He had managed to get just a couple of steps before turning around, pulling me into his arms again, and kissing me once more. That was the moment I had awakened.

There was a profound sense of happiness in my soul and a huge smile on my face. I bounced out of bed, filled with tons of joyful energy.

I just knew that today would be absolutely amazing, and someday soon, such a passionate love would be mine!

My morning routine was completed in record time since I was in a rush. It was just a few minutes before I entered the living area of our suite. Richard was already awake. He always got up early, just the opposite of me, who worked late into the night and then slept in.

"Good morning, my brother dearest!" I announced cheerfully before giving him a hug.

"Aren't you in a joyful mood! That rest must have done you a world of good! I take it that for once you actually went straight to sleep?" he inquired.

"I did! I was out like a light and had some wonderful dreams! Are you ready to go kayaking today?" I questioned, grabbing his hand and impatiently pulling him towards the door. We were both laughing by the time we reached the dining room. The feeling of utter and complete happiness inside me seemed to be infectious!

Breakfast was just as good as the day before, but today, the young waiter brought each of us a glass of fresh-pressed orange juice. After handing Richard his glass, Jeffrey offered mine to me with a flourish.

"May I present this special glass of juice to our beloved princess?" he declared.

I smiled at Jeffrey's antics and accepted the glass with a smile. "Thank you, kind sir! I am sure that I will enjoy this special juice immensely!"

All three of us ended up laughing. Neither Richard nor I realized at the time, how much truth had been in those joking words! We thought he was just playing.

Since we were going to try to kayak around a good part of the island, my brother and I ate a healthy breakfast. We drank every last drop of our orange juice. We had never tasted a beverage so full of flavor, so alive, and it surprised both Richard and me. How could simple juice possibly taste so good?

⊱✿⊰

Even after having been there for just a short time, we felt that we had truly hit the jackpot with this place. The accommodations were magnificent, the food out of this world, and the service superb as well as fun. We seemed to be the only guests and loved having the whole place to ourselves.

The next couple of days were just wonderful. Richard and I were having a fabulous time. During the day, we were off enjoying all kinds of adventures, in the evenings, we had leisurely dinners and talked. This was really the first chance I had in years to deeply connect with my brother, and I was cherishing every moment.

The love we had shared since early childhood grew stronger, and we discovered all kinds of things about each other we had never known. I was truly grateful to have this amazing opportunity. It was wonderful to get to spend time with the one sibling closest to me.

I could still barely fathom the luck which had brought us to such a remarkable and fun spot. We had looked at several hotels but had never imagined that a place such as this even existed!

The theme of the resort was 'Scottish Highlands of Old,' and the costumes of the staff were absolutely stunning. Since this sort of setting was right up my alley, I absolutely loved the ambiance. Most of my stories are set in similar time periods. This hotel was so authentic in most aspects that it was almost like living back then. I was observing and accumulating all kinds of ideas for my next books.

In addition, I felt more at home on the island every day. I had observed this with some curiosity. Since I felt so inspired here, I was actually considering looking at houses in the village. Yes, it was closer to the earthquake fault, but on the other hand, all the buildings were sitting on solid rock instead of glacial till, and the danger zone was the same as for my present residence.

Why was this island drawing me so? Did it have something to do with the vivid dreams I continued to have each night? They were always of the same man, and by now, I was totally in love with him. If I could only find such an amazing man in real life!

Every time I thought of him, deep yearning filled my heart and soul. I was no longer staying up to work until late, as was my usual habit. Instead, I took some time during the day to edit my book.

I usually could not wait to go to sleep once the sun had set and went straight to bed when we got back to our suite. Those nights spent with this amazing dream man became as real to me as Richard's and my adventures during the day.

Most of my books are fantasy or fantasy love stories. I think being able to escape into a reality far removed from everyday life is a magical thing, yet another reason this island appealed to me so very much!

I loved wearing my long, beautiful gowns for dinner. Dressing up like a medieval lady fed my inner princess and just somehow felt right. The conclusion I came to was that I must have lived during that time.

The contrast between night and day was also fun. For the hiking and kayaking my brother and I were doing, we wore shorts and casual shirts. At night, however, I donned my fine garb and became a lady of times long past. Richard wore a dark suit; he was not getting into the dress-up spirit quite as much as I was.

Our stay was affecting him in other ways, even if he refused to dress like the rest of the men. My brother was very gallant at the best of times, but being here had brought out even more of his chivalry. We were both enjoying ourselves immensely in this world of make-believe.

⚜

On the sixth day of our stay, the weather was perfect for sailing. To my delight, the resort made several small sailboats available to its guests. Richard and I had discovered these the day we had gone out kayaking. I had been impatiently waiting for just the right amount of wind ever since.

My brother does not share my passion for being out on the water, especially not in a small sailboat. He decided that he would stay behind on shore and read a book. He would be right there so that he could keep a watch on me just in case of the unlikely event that I got myself into trouble.

One of the staff members rigged the boat for me and showed me how to use it. Soon I was happily gliding through the gentle waves. Sailing is one of my biggest loves, and I was delighted to be rapidly zipping along in the waters just off the island.

I kept adjusting the sails and my course to take maximum advantage of the wind. I love going fast, and the more speed I managed to squeeze out of the small boat, the more delighted I was. The little vessel was amazingly fast. How exhilarating!

⁕

Being an experienced sailor, I had asked about the tide before heading out. I had no desire to get into trouble. In some areas, the water between the islands streamed like fast-flowing rivers. A little boat such as this would be helpless against a current flowing several knots, and I had no intention to allow myself to be swept away.

I noticed that it was pretty gusty at times, definitely a challenge. I would have to be careful and remain on alert. Out here, it was just me pitching myself against mother nature. I absolutely loved it but was not taking needless chances. The sun on my face, a breeze in my hair, being out on the water! Perfect!

⁕

Around noon, the wind died down, and my little boat slowed to a crawl. Since I no longer had to be so attentive, I started looking around more as I drifted closer to shore. At first, my eyes slid right over the barely perceptible figure sitting high up there on the rocks watching me, but suddenly, something registered. My eyes snapped back to the spot.

Turning my head slightly so it did not appear as if I was investigating the area more closely, I examined every foot of the rock. There! I had been right, there was someone up there! And he or she was very well camouflaged! What was that all about? That would definitely bear keeping an eye on. I decided that for now, I would not reveal that I had noticed that I was being observed.

I could just barely make out the outline of a person, but I was absolutely certain that someone was up there. My gut confirmed what my eyes had already told me. How long had he or she been there, and why were they hiding? And, who was it? I would definitely keep a closer watch on my surroundings from now on!

༴ས༺

The morning's sail had been positively thrilling at times. I took advantage of the lull during the noon hour to eat the lunch I had brought with me. Soon enough, the wind picked back up, and I enjoyed another couple of hours of exhilarating sailing.

Besides writing, being on the water was definitely one activity that was my bliss. For me, nothing compared to silently gliding through the water with the sun sparkling on its surface, to being one with the elements.

The sound of the sails, the creaking of the mast, the wind singing in the rigging, it filled me with pure joy and happiness. Andrew and I had sailed a lot. How much I missed it! Maybe it was time I bought my own boat?

I longed to be back out on the deep ocean, away from it all. On the way to Hawaii, on an especially calm day, I had seen the sea look like a smooth lake. It had been of a deep blue color that was incomparable to anything else.

To me, it had been a magical journey that had given birth to my vivid dreams. I had loved having the dawn all to myself, a thousand miles from any shore. Being on the water always made me feel so very free.

༴ས༺

I could have continued to sail all day, but I figured that Richard would be getting bored before long, so I reluctantly headed back towards shore. I had been warned that the wind would die down later in the afternoon. It was much better to coast in than to have to paddle from this far out, especially in a vessel not designed for such a thing!

The figure up on the rocks was still there but had moved into the shade a while ago. Got hot, did he? Served him right for sneakily watching me! Then it occurred to me. Was this the resort's way of unobtrusively keeping an eye on their guests? Somehow I thought this quite possible. The staff was always very discreet.

Whatever was the case, I was not going to do anything about this unless it became a threat. I can handle myself, which makes me good at ignoring things when I chose to. I also decided not to mention being observed to Richard. He would just end up worrying and sticking to me like glue.

⚜

At some point during my sail, I had taken to thinking of my observer as he. It made more sense to me somehow than thinking that it was a woman up there on that rock keeping an eye out. And, the vibrations I had detected were definitely male.

I had prowlers before, and each and every one of them had been a guy. Usually, they had gotten tired of not getting a rise out of me and, after a while, had faded away. Also, installing more cameras and having a big dog had helped to deter further intrusions into my yard. My German Shepherd had no sense of humor when it came to anyone sneaking about!

I had concluded that on one hand, it was kind of creepy being watched like this, but on the other, it made me feel safe. If I got tipped over by a sudden strong gust of wind, at least there was someone besides Richard to see it. My gut told me that all was well, and that was what mattered to me.

⚜

My brother and the guy who had rigged the boat were waiting for me on the shore. I waved to them happily as I got closer. Dropping the mainsail, I slowed down the little boat enough to keep it from racing into the small bay used as a sort of harbor. Just before reaching the beach, I let down the foresail and expertly coasted the rest of the way in.

"Well done!" shouted Richard. "It looked like you had a great time out there! I was not sure you were ever going to come in!" he finished with a laugh.

"Miss me, did you?" I replied, giving him a hug. It was wonderful to be so loved. My brother was the one person I could always turn to, no matter what. He would do just about anything for me and me for him.

⁕⁕⁕

I felt amazing after that sail. Relaxed, peaceful, exhilarated, and filled to overflowing with pure joyfulness. The sun was warm on my skin, and the wind was caressing my shoulder-length hair. A feeling of utter and complete wellbeing filled me from head to toe.

Having been out there, just me and the boat against the wind and sea, had made me feel incredibly alive. Every nerve in my body was strumming with boundless energy. Being on this island, on vacation, and far away from all the worries of home, seemed to be doing me a world of good.

Here, there were no fans clamoring for my attention, no pesky admirers to fend off, no marketing to deal with, no garden to weed and bushes to trim, no house to look after. I missed my pets, but not having to worry about all the rest just felt marvelous. I could get used to this!

Would living on this island always make me feel like this? Would being removed from the busy world to such an isolated place help or hinder my craft? My stories wanted to be told, to be shared with my readers. I would have to think about that.

⁕⁕⁕

After grabbing my bag out of the boat, Richard and I headed back towards the resort. I was starving. Being on the water always made me hungry, and today I was plain ravenous.

My brother and I shared an early dinner. As usual, the food was fabulous. This night, we were served salmon in a caper sauce with just a hint of lemon, salt potatoes tossed in butter, and green asparagus. We each had a glass of wine

~ 63 ~

with our meal and decided that we deserved a desert when our waiter told us about the gluten-free cheesecake the chef had made especially for us.

Tonight, however, there would be no sitting outside watching the sun go down. As predicted, the wind had let up a bit in the afternoon but had started truly howling later that day. The terrace was being swept by ferocious gusts. We could hear the sound of the waves beating against the rocks far below, even over the soft music playing in the room.

Richard and I lingered in front of the fireplace in the great room for a while. We had set up a scrabble board but, somehow, neither one of us managed to get into the spirit of the game.

We finally decided to call it an early evening and headed for our suite.

Chapter 8

Longing

Richard and I hugged and said goodnight once we got back to our suite. We each headed to our room. I was tired but also excited. Would that gorgeous hunk of a dream man be waiting for me? I so very much hoped so! One night, he had shown me Paris, the next Rome. Then, we had visited London. As much as I enjoyed seeing all these places, I would have so much rather explored somewhere quiet if it meant being alone with him.

I still had not seen his face clearly, but his mannerisms and build had been burned into my memory. His voice, when he called my name, was like a caress, his hands when he touched me, sent electric shocks through my system. I wanted to touch him and be touched, I longed to be held by him, to actually wake up in his arms.

If only he were real! I knew that he loved me. How amazing life would be together with him! He was the kind of man who made a woman feel safe and cherished. I would never have to protect myself from him like I have had to do in the past from other partners.

This guy was everything I had ever dreamed of, and it was getting harder and harder to not show my impatience to get an evening over with. Once the sun started to set, I just wanted to head to bed as quickly as possible so that I could be with him.

Richard deserved my full attention! I felt that it was not fair of me to cut the time I spent with my brother short for a man I had only met in my dreams, no matter how much my heart and soul longed for this gorgeous hunk during the day.

⋰⋰⋰⋰⋰

My dreams had always been extremely vivid, but nothing like this. I actually felt his touch, smelled his scent as well as the odors of the places we visited, could clearly hear his voice as well as those of the people around us. Sometimes it almost seemed that the time with him was more real than my waking hours. To me, this was all very confusing.

Of one thing I was sure by now. As ridiculous as it sounded, I was in love with this man and deeply so. What would happen once I left the island? Would I stop dreaming of him?

I could not imagine a life without being held in his arms, even if it was just in a dream. It would break my heart to lose him, to never see him again. That was how much a part of my world he had already become. I realized that I would stay on this island forever just to remain together with him.

⋰⋰⋰⋰⋰

Just the thought of what I was willing to do for a man I had only met in my nightly adventures filled me with fear as well as anger. When had I become so desperate, so lonely that I would go to such length just to feel loved? This was totally not like me. What was going on?

I was usually pretty levelheaded and realized that dreams were just that - dreams! When had I changed so much that I longed to linger in an alternate world? None of this made any sense to me anymore.

I decided that I would allow myself to enjoy the dreams, but it was time to get a grip. This insane longing for a man I had never actually met just had to go! After all, how could I fulfill my life's purpose of channeling tales if I was more interested in living in a fairytale world myself?

I love my gift. Telling stories is more than a calling for me, it is my absolute bliss. It is as important to me as breathing and part of my very being. My tales usually start with a dream and then just flow from my fingertips. At times I can barely keep up with those nimble digits flying over the keys.

Right then and there, I decided that my dream lover and I would have to have a chat. Things could not continue like this. I wanted him in my life, not lead a shadow existence! Having made up my mind to confront the situation, I fell peacefully asleep.

That night, he wanted to show me the pyramids, but I told him flat out that I wanted to talk first. Since we were already in Egypt, we looked for a sand dune that allowed us a nice view of the surrounding landscape. From where we were, we could just barely make out the river Nile in the distance.

Once we found the ideal spot, my love produced two comfortable chairs, a small table with an umbrella, and a carafe of what looked like fresh-squeezed lemonade. For some reason, this seemed perfectly normal to me. This was a dream, after all. Once we were comfortably seated, he turned to me.

"What would you like to talk about? I realize that for you to turn down a tour of the pyramids, the subject must be important to you!"

"I love you showing me the world, and I love being with you. I am also becoming very used to our life together in this fashion. That is what scares me. I find myself missing you during the day and wanting to rush off to bed just to be near you. To be honest, I find my own desire, my need for you very disturbing. Will we ever be together for real?"

My companion studied me intensely. "Do you love me?" he asked after a moment. I saw the tension in him as he was waiting for my answer. Ever so gently, I reached out my hand and touched his beautiful face. To me, he was the most gorgeous man alive. No other would ever be able to come even close to the attraction I felt for my stunning, kind, and so very attentive dream lover.

"Yes, I love you. Enough to contemplate staying on this island to be near you! That is not like me! What about my writing? My stories need to be told!" I responded honestly.

The smile that stole across his face at my words rivaled the sun. His eyes lit up with happiness. Never in my life had I seen someone go from pensive to floating on cloud nine in just a few moments, and just because I had told him that he had won my heart! This was definitely a first for me.

Next thing I knew, I found myself pulled up into his arms, and his mouth was descending on mine. The weakness that spread through my body made me cling to him all the more. What would it feel like to experience this in real life? I bet it would be just indescribable!

When we finally came up for air, we were both panting rapidly. I felt like I had just run a marathon and could barely catch my breath. My pulse was racing, and my legs felt too weak to support me. This had been an incredible kiss!

"Do you trust me?" he asked after a moment, looking deep into my eyes. There was such love, such warmth, such passion and longing in these beautiful orbs that my heart constricted for a moment, and I could not find my voice.

Never in my life had a man looked at me like this, wanted me this badly, loved me this much. This was the relationship I had wished for all my life! Would it always be just a dream?

THAT would be heartbreaking, that was for sure. I longed to be loved, to be wanted, to be desired in the same measure I felt for my man.

Until this moment, this exquisite feeling had eluded me. I had known that having my love returned in equal measure would feel amazing, but I had not been prepared for the true ecstasy of such a union.

When I could finally speak, I answered him from the heart, "I trust you, totally and completely, but the feeling we share is terrifying as well. I never imagined that it could feel so all-consuming!"

"It does feel incredible, doesn't it? Soon, I will be with you, and we will never be parted again. You will have me all day long, and I will hold you in my arms all night. I will make passionate love to you; I will adore you and love you like you have never been loved before. Can you wait just a few more days?" came his response.

I could feel the truth in his words, and I was beyond happiness. We would be together, for real! My heart started singing with joy. To have him by my side, to wake up to him in the mornings, to be held when I needed his closeness, to love and be loved, and to have this for a lifetime was a dream come true!

What were a few more days when such bliss awaited me? I smiled up at him radiantly. "I can wait. I have waited long enough for you to find me. A few more days is nothing in the scheme of things! As long as I know that we will be together, all is well with my world!"

My love pulled me tightly against him. I could feel his heart beating and relaxed into his embrace. Here was the place I belonged; I was home!

Being held felt so good that I could have stayed in his arms forever, but we were in a magical place, and it would have been a shame to leave those beckoning pyramids unexplored.

"Well, my love, are you ready for me to show you the wonders of Egypt?" he finally asked me. I nodded into the loose shirt covering that pleasingly hard chest. In response, I could feel him place a tender kiss on my hair.

"Well, darling, let's be off! There is much to be seen!" he whispered into my ear before gently giving my earlobe a quick but sensual lick.

That brief touch of his tongue sent delicious shivers down my entire body. I could not wait to make love to this man, but for now, Egypt would have to do!

Chapter 9

A Rainy Day

I awoke the next morning with an incredible sense of wellbeing and of being cherished. What a wonderful dream! The pyramids had been truly fascinating. I loved the ornate burial chambers and wished that I could read the hieroglyphs painted everywhere. The sphinx had made me wonder what was hidden in all that sand around it.

My love and I had wandered hand in hand through magnificent tombs, and he had taken me places regular tourists never did get to see, one of the advantages of traveling in spirit form. What a delightful adventure we ended up having!

I was looking forward to this evening and curious about where we would end up this time. Every night was a surprise. I just loved exploring all those places I had never been to before but had wanted to see for as long as I could remember. I had dropped a hint about Norway to my thoughtful companion. Stretching leisurely in my bed, I was wondering if that would be our next destination.

***

Our waiter, Jeffrey, had mentioned the night before that we were most likely in for a change in the weather. When it was gusty like that, he had told us, it usually heralded a storm coming in. Sure enough, I could hear the rain beating against my windows, and the wind was still howling outside.

Since we would not be doing anything outside while it was pouring like this, I snuggled underneath the covers for a few minutes longer reveling in the afterglow of my fabulous dream. I could not wait to feel that gorgeous man's arms around me for real!

***

Just a few more days, and we would be together forever! My heart was singing with happiness. I would finally experience the love I had known could exist and had written about but had never tasted. Right then and there, I felt truly blessed, and like the luckiest woman alive.

I allowed myself to dwell on the fun-filled night for a while longer then bounced out of bed. I felt like hugging the entire world and dancing out there in the rain. Joy filled every bit of my being, but how could I possibly explain to my brother why I was elated like this?

I had not shared my dreams with Richard. Somehow, they had felt too private to divulge to anyone. Time with my companion was special to me, and falling in love with a guy in one's dreams did sound like insanity even to me. Better to keep quiet about all this for now. I was sure that the two main men in my life would meet soon enough.

Feeling ecstatically happy, I quickly completed my morning routine. Richard was seated comfortably in one of the chairs reading when I entered our living area.

"Good morning, brother dearest!" I greeted him before bouncing over to give him a hug. Richard eyed me curiously.

"My, are we in a good mood on such a rainy day. Sleep well or something?" he asked me with a smile.

"I slept wonderfully! How about you? Are you ready for breakfast? And what are we doing today?" I asked in rapid succession.

Richard started laughing. "What are we going to do with all that excess energy? I hope we can find some sort of an outlet! And yes, I slept well, and I am ready for breakfast! Shall we?"

"Sorry, I can't help myself! I just feel so amazing today! For some reason, I am totally and utterly happy and feel that something wonderful is about to happen!"

"That is one thing I love to hear! Your intuitions are usually right on, so I can't wait to see what is coming our way! But, first things first! Let's go have some breakfast and coffee. Not that I think you need any! You might bounce right out the window if you wire up even more!" Richard declared. He was laughing while holding the door to our suite open for me.

⋆⋅☆⋅⋆

The dining room was ready for us, as usual. This was our seventh day at the resort and my brother, and I absolutely loved the place. If at all possible, we intended to come back the next year. We both felt that this was an amazing place, a real find.

I had, however, noticed that something was a bit odd about some of the inhabitants of the beautiful island. They were all very friendly and treated us like royalty, but they were also proud and very mysterious and mostly kept to themselves. When we were out and about, we practically had most of the island to ourselves.

How this was even possible in this day and age was beyond us. People loved the San Juans, and all the other islands were getting more and more crowded with each passing year. This must be the largest privately held isle left in the entire area!

A Rainy Day

In the past, Richard and I had stayed at some expensive hotels but never in any place as unique as this. The feeling of having stepped back into a slower and more peaceful time was pervasive, and the staff at the hotel were definitely different from most other resorts he and I had stayed at.

✦⊱≺⊱⊰≻⊰✦

After another sumptuous breakfast and two cups of the delicious coffee, one hazelnut, and one caramel, we were trying to decide what to do with ourselves. Since it was still raining outside, hiking and all the other outside sports were out. Richard inquired of our waiter if he had any suggestions.

We were both surprised by the available selection. Neither one of us had expected such a variety to choose from. Since it was fairly early, we decided that we could manage to pack several activities into our day.

We would begin with fencing lessons, then brush up on our ballroom dancing. After lunch, we would spend some time with the local fortuneteller, followed by more fencing. A séance was scheduled for after dinner. Now that was something I had never attended before!

To our surprise, we were told that much of the entertainment offered to the guests during rainy or blustery days was of some sort of paranormal nature. All the activities were designed to reinforce the mysterious and medieval atmosphere of the resort.

Since I had been reading cards as well as people most of my life, this was right up my alley. I decided to take full advantage of the available activities, and Richard was only too happy to join me. Our shared interests in such things were only one of the reasons that he is my favorite brother!

✦⊱≺⊱⊰≻⊰✦

This island was really just too perfect for me, almost like a dream! It gave my fantasy wings, and at times, I expected knights to come charging around the corner at any moment or a dragon to appear in the sky. I would not have been surprised to come across a unicorn in one of the meadows or meet up with fairies and elves. There was just something magical about this place!

My sixth sense, however, continued to tingle. I was not sure what was setting it off but had every intention of finding out. I had noticed that even away from the resort, some of the people were wearing old fashioned garb. Somehow I found it odd that the entire island would maintain the resort's theme.

Our usual waiter, Jeffrey, was really nice and I had been asking him plenty of questions. He had been only too happy to tell us about his home. We had found out that the community on the island consisted of several artists as well as some very successful businessmen. Some were only here on the weekends or in the summer, others stayed all year long.

Also, the resort was not always this empty. We had been lucky that the group which had booked the rest of the hotel had canceled at the last moment. Later in August, the hotel hosted an artist retreat as well as a renaissance fair.

During those days, the island was usually overrun with people, but, according to Jefferey, most of the inhabitants preferred the quiet to all the influx of visitors. And, they liked the theme of the resort.

This explained some of the peculiarities, but not all. Of the people we had come across, only a few wore modern garb. My brother and I had seen a couple young girls in shorts or short skirts, but most of the time, the ladies wore the beautiful time period gowns.

The men, when not working, were also impeccably dressed. Somehow this all seemed fun, but a bit much. I don't know if I would want to run around in a long dress all year long!

⚜

One thing I had come to understand: there was something very special about this island! The woods felt full of mysteries, and I expected to run into something unusual at every moment. And then, there were the megaliths! My brother and I had been so busy that we had yet to go back to the stone circle. I think Richard had been stalling since he was leery of the power we had both felt emanating from within.

A couple of times during our hikes, we had felt like we were being watched. But, we had never seen anyone following us. Could it have been the same man who had been up there on the rocks? Maybe I could sneak up on him? That was definitely a question to ponder some other day. Now, it was time to have fun!

⁖⁖⁖

I took to fencing like a fish to water, and within a short time, Richard was hard-pressed to fend off my attacks. We had such a good time that we pushed ballroom dancing off to the afternoon. Both of us were dripping with sweat and needed a shower before we could go to lunch.

Jeffrey greeted us as we entered the dining room. He was unusually talkative today and regaled us with all kinds of stories about the island's present and past inhabitants. He soon had us laughing so hard I ended up having to hold my sides.

The food was delicious, as always. The chef had prepared a hearty beef soup since the weather was so inclement outside. And, he had made a gluten-free key lime pie! Another one of my favorite treats I had been missing! I could not remember the last time I had eaten a piece. Therefore, I ended up having two!

⁖⁖⁖

Both Richard and I had learned to ballroom dance in our youth. We now got a welcome refresher. One of the maids partnered Richard while Jeffrey insisted on dancing with me. One thing became obvious very quickly. Our waiter loved to dance!

We started out with a sedate Waltz. It did not take me long to remember the steps. The Cha-Cha-Cha was a little more challenging, and after we had mastered that, we moved on to the Tango. Now there was a dance I hoped to share with my love very soon, but for now, Jefferey would do!

The music and the dancing really stirred my blood, especially when the memory of being held close to that well-muscled chest came to mind. I was also fascinated by my dream lover's incredible hands with those long slender fingers.

Those remarkable digits possessed a dexterity, power, and strength that took my breath away. I had to wrench my thoughts back to the moment when I missed a step and bumped into Jeffrey.

The rest of the lesson, I kept my mind firmly planted in the present. Thinking of my love was just too much of a distraction and best to be done when I was not otherwise occupied!

Marie, the maid, had made quite an impression on Richard. She was not just a member of the staff at the resort but also a talented artist. She played piano, violin, as well as the flute and had performed all over the world. Her job at the hotel was more to fill the time than out of a need for the money.

⁘⁘⁘

Eventually, it was time to meet up with the fortune teller. My brother had been rather reluctant to part with his dancing partner. I had watched with amusement as he was doing his best to keep her talking just a few minutes longer. Marie seemed equally smitten. I did not miss the gentle touch to Richard's chest before I finally managed to drag him away.

To our delight, the lady who was doing the reading was dressed in an elaborate gypsy costume, all very authentic and fun! She greeted us just outside the suite designated especially for these kinds of activities and invited us in. It even had a sign on the door stating, 'Welcome to the World of Magic!'

I let Richard go in first. If this person had the gift, I suspected that he would get welcome news. While I waited, I watched the rain and wind raging around the hotel. Was it my imagination or had it gotten worse?

The minutes ticked by, and I looked around the suite a bit more. It was just like Richard's and mine with two rooms and a central living space where I now waited. But unlike our area, this one was decorated to give off a mystical and magical air.

This place was so whimsical, so spiritual, and cleverly done. It disguised the real purpose of some of the decorations of granting protection! I could not help but examine the crystals, windchimes, and tapestries more closely. I absolutely loved it, and I was gathering ideas for my own home.

⁘

The reading was taking much longer than I had anticipated. Finally, my brother came out. He was beaming. The seeress was good! She had told Richard what I already knew: there was romance in his future!

I had not missed the sparkle in my brother's eye nor the skip in his step since our dancing lesson. When he spoke of Marie, his entire expression softened and took on a dreamy, hopeful look. I had been thrilled to hear that he had invited her to join us for a glass of wine after the séance and that she had accepted.

⁘

After a few more minutes, the gypsy opened the door and waved me in. It was my turn. I entered the room and was surprised by the effort that had been made to make it look just like a real tent. Pastel-colored scarves lent the whole thing a very mystical atmosphere. This was absolutely fabulous and truly set the stage for a magical experience.

The fortuneteller introduced herself as Angelique. She was very gracious and quite beautiful in her colorful outfit. I quickly came to the conclusion that this seeress was no fake. The ethereal air she had about her told me that she had a genuine connection to the Divine.

Once I sat down across the table from her, the lady and I locked eyes for a moment. Suddenly, I could see hers go blank. Interesting! What exactly was going on here? A faraway look had come over the gypsy's features while she slowly shuffled the tarot cards.

Once again, the seeress predicted romance but also a significant change in circumstances as well as a move not far into the future. She saw incredible success for my books and a long, happy life. I was good with all that! Then, she suddenly grabbed my hands and turned them over to see my lifeline.

"Do you know what you are?" she asked me. All I could do was look at her, stunned. I had no idea what she was talking about. "No, I do not," I answered.

"You think you almost died, do you not?" came the next question. "Yes, a few years ago," I answered, now truly puzzled.

My life had changed drastically after that incident. For one, my will to live had been born and a burning desire to get out of the situation I found myself in, to be able to walk again, and to live on my own. I had achieved those goals within three years.

"You did die, but you came back, you came back as more. Your life will never again be as it was," the seeress explained. "You, you are truly blessed, do not forget that, ever!" she finished.

With those words, the blank look left the gypsy's face, and she smiled at me. "You will be very happy, child. Stay the innocent, fey creature you are. Never let anyone change you! Remember, you are beautiful, just as you are!"

Who was she calling child? She was younger than I was! Or at least, she looked that way. Dropping my shields for a moment, I was surprised by the ancient feeling of the seeress's spirit. There was much more to this woman than I had first thought! I found myself genuinely liking her.

"Thank you, Angelique! I am looking forward to the future you have predicted! And, you have given me much to think about! I am grateful for your insights!" I told her sincerely.

"You are most welcome," the seeress answered, smiling. She rose gracefully and guided me out the door to the sitting area where my brother was waiting. This had definitely been an interesting experience!

Richard and I both thanked the lady again, and I watched as he slipped her a couple of bills. She must have really impressed him because I could have sworn they were hundreds!

Dinner was delicious, as always. This time, the chef had prepared steaks with a mixed salad and vegetables. Everything tasted wonderful, especially the Crème Brule that followed the meal! How could this man possibly know all my favorite deserts? I gave Richard a suspicious look, and he smiled. I should have known!

I could not help but hug him! Leave it to my ever-thoughtful brother to make sure that I got the treats I missed out on so often due to my gluten intolerance! How could one not love such an amazing man? Any woman he ended up with would be truly a very lucky lady!

The séance was held in the second chamber of the wonderfully magical suite. The room was lit only with candles, and a large, round table had been placed in the center. Marie, Jeffrey, the cook as well as the Maître d' had joined us. The seeress, Angelique, would preside over the meeting.

I was not sure how I felt about contacting the dead, but my curiosity was greater than my apprehension. The gypsy would be the one leading us, and my gut told me that she could be trusted. Once we were all seated around the table, she had everyone clasp hands and close their eyes.

Richard was on my left with Marie on his other side. George, the cook, was on her far side and Allan across from her. Jeffrey had claimed the chair to my right. The six of us had been pretty excited because you truly never knew what to expect during one of these events.

Angelique was quite the presence as she sat there between George and Allan. There was no doubt in anyone's mind that she was completely in charge. After asking us if we were all ready to begin, the gypsy spoke a brief prayer asking for protection. Then, she began calling to those residing beyond the veil.

﹏﹏❀﹏﹏

I had no idea what to expect, but I was not prepared for the sudden drop in temperature. It seemed that none of us were for I could hear gasps all around. My eyes flew open. The seeress' eyes had rolled back in her head and were pure white. A silvery mist was emanating from her mouth, followed by a deep voice that addressed each one of us, one after the other.

The spirit had a detailed communication for everyone present. I was given a tender message from my deceased mother, and I could feel her love surround me with her very first words. She told me that she was so very proud of me and to believe and trust my instincts. Everything would work out beautifully.

I was grateful for those assurances as well as the contact with my mom. It was nice to know that all had been forgiven on both sides and that now only love existed between us. While she was alive, things had not always been that way.

Richard received a similar message. Mom told him that his cancer would not return and that his health would continue to improve. And, he would end up marrying the love of his life. My brother was so happy that he was beaming at Marie who was smiling back at him.

﹏﹏❀﹏﹏

Allan, the maître d' had just received his message, and I could see tears in his eyes. Life would be looking up for him as well. In a few weeks, he would meet a wonderful lady and fall deeply in love.

All was very serene and peaceful until suddenly the voice shouted: "It is coming! Beware! Be..."

The medium's last words were cut off abruptly, and she collapsed in her chair. Letting go of my neighbors' hands, I immediately rushed to her side. Just as I reached her, a sudden wind rushed through the room, blowing out all but a couple of the candles.

Even in the dim light, I could tell that Angelique's breathing was shallow and uneven. She was covered in sweat and deeply unconscious. "Smelling salts! Do you have any smelling salts or ammonia?" I had to shout to make myself heard. Everyone in the room was confused and a little scared.

Something momentous had happened or was about to. None of us knew what to expect. Only the seeress might be able to figure out what was going on. But, to get answers, we needed to bring her around!

⁘⁓⁕⁃

My attempts to get some help were in vain. I finally had it and smacked my hand on the table, hard. The sound echoed through the room and, just as intended, got everyone's attention.

After that, it took me only a moment to organize the lot. Marie and Richard went off to find smelling salts of some sort, Jeffrey went to fetch a wet washcloth, the cook I sent off for some kind of spirits.

My gut told me that we needed to figure this out fast. There was a sudden great urgency inside me that I had managed to get across to the rest. Within minutes, we had succeeded in reviving the seeress.

⁘⁓⁕⁃

Angelique now sat at the table, shaking like a leaf. I had placed a blanket around her, but she was still freezing.

We needed to get her warmed up and calmed down. The cook pressed a glass of cognac into her hands. Maybe the alcohol would help.

The gypsy tossed the amber liquid down in one gulp, holding her glass out for more. I let her have one more drink, then got her attention.

"Are you doing better?" I asked her with concern. All she could do was nod. "I am so sorry, but we need to know what to expect. I would not put you through this right now if I did not feel that this was of the utmost importance. What is coming? Can you tell us, please?"

For a moment, the lady looked inward than she blanched even more. I would not have believed this possible because she had already been deathly white. "A storm! A storm is coming! A bad one! And soon! We need to prepare!" she gasped. "The basement! You need to get to the basement! Warn the other residents!"

With those words, the exhausted seeress lost consciousness once more. The maître d' and I exchanged concerned glances.

Whatever was coming, it sure did not sound good!

Chapter 10

The Storm

We were all stunned for a moment after the seeress' revelation. A storm? And a bad one? From the maître d's face, it was obvious that he had not been aware of the incoming tempest, but the capable man immediately took charge. A flurry of activities ensued.

All Richard's and my things were quickly and competently packed up and hauled into the basement, as were our mattresses, sheets, and covers. Within minutes, the staff had created a cozy space separated by blankets for each of us. Other residents from all over the island started to arrive and were settled in equally as efficient.

In the meantime, the storm outside had quieted. The sky had turned an eerie shade of green, and an oppressive silence was hanging over the area.

Something was definitely coming! Figuring that I would be stuck down in that basement with all those people for a while, I decided to take the opportunity to slip outside for a little.

꘏꘏꘏

Richard was helping Marie. I assumed that he would be too busy to notice my departure from the basement, but my intention of heading up the stairs was not missed by the sharp eyes of the maître d'. Realizing that Allan was watching me, I walked over to him.

"I need some air before the storm hits. Do you mind if I head outside for a bit now that it has stopped raining?" I asked him.

The usually a little reserved man eyed me with curiosity. "Too many people down here for you, eh?" the observant maître d' commented with a smile.

"Please, just be careful and stay close. I have no idea what to expect, but I am preparing this place for the worst. By the way, thank you for your help after the séance! I was a bit rattled by the whole thing, especially that strange gust of wind and the lights going out so suddenly!"

"You are most welcome," I answered, returning his smile. "I will be back in a little while."

꘏꘏꘏

I felt much better once I was outside. Taking deep breaths, I carefully looked around me. Had it not been for my close scrutiny, I would have missed the figure slipping into the shadows just as I was turning that way.

It was getting close to sundown, but there had been plenty of light left to notice him. Was this my mysterious watcher from the rock again? It sure felt like it! What an opportunity!

My mind immediately started to come up with plans. Now that it was just he and I out here, I might finally be able to confront my shadow! How could I draw him out into the open? Where could I go so that he would have to reveal himself when he followed?

I needed someplace open with a hiding place but close by so that I was not getting too far away from the buildings.

After evaluating my surroundings, I decided on the nearby pasture. All the horses had been brought in, so I was sure no one would mind me exploring in there.

A big tree on top of a small hill was perfect for what I had in mind. I could saunter along towards it, then dash behind it and be able to watch for anyone following me.

My shadow should reasonably assume that I had continued on my way. I liked my plan; it was the best I could come up with under the circumstances and on such short notice. My pursuer would have to cross an open area to reach me.

❦

Within minutes, I was carefully concealed behind the large tree. Sure enough! A man detached himself from the buildings and headed my way. Just as I had hoped, he must have assumed that I had gone on! The closer he got, the more familiar he seemed. The grace of his movements, his tall, well-muscled frame, all sparked to life a fuzzy memory.

Who was this guy? He seemed familiar, but I could not place him. One thing I did know for sure, I had not seen him at the hotel! I would have remembered his mannerisms. This man moved with the grace and the caution of a wild animal, a wolf perhaps. Suddenly, he stopped and then, he was gone. How was that possible?

I stayed where I was and kept looking around, but I could not locate him. It was getting too dark for me to be out here much longer, so I started heading back towards the manor. On the way, I stopped and carefully examined the last place I had seen my shadow.

The only clue I could find made no sense to me at that time whatsoever. In the fading light, I could just barely make out a man's barefoot print, but the one next to it was of some sort of a very large canine!

The pawprint was huge, almost as big as my hand! Very mysterious but also quite scary! I hurried towards the hotel since I did not relish the thought of being out there alone in the twilight with an unknown as well as enormous creature!

⸎

By the time I returned to the basement, things had settled down a bit. The maître d' acknowledged me with a nod, and I headed for my cubicle. I was at the furthest end of the cellar, near one of the closed-off outside exits, with only Richard beside me. My brother was in his own space. I could hear him talk softly with Marie. Just as I had intuited, those two were sure hitting it off!

The thought that my cherished sibling had finally found a loving companion made me happy. He had been through much the last few years and deserved some happiness. Maybe coming here had been a great thing for us both!

In the small space allotted to me, my pajamas had been laid out on the bed. It might be just a mattress on the floor, but the staff had done their best to make the cubicle as homey as possible.

A light had been placed on a small table, my clothes were neatly hung up on a rack or stacked on temporary shelves, the bed was nicely made and turned down as usual. All the comforts of home without the room!

⸎

"May I enter?" came a quiet voice from the other side of the curtain.

Since I was still decent and had not yet gotten ready for bed, I responded. "Yes, you may."

The maître d' was making his rounds to make sure everyone was as comfortable as possible and ready to settle in for the night. Allan told me that the overhead lights would be turned off in just a few minutes. All of us needed to get as much sleep as possible before the storm hit. When that would be was everyone's best guess.

The circumspect man had given a briefing to all the other temporary residents of our shelter, but having been off on my own adventure, I had missed it. He showed me where to find the toilet and the place to wash up and brush my teeth. I thanked him for his kindness and then set off to quickly attend to an abbreviated evening routine.

✦✧❀✧✦

I had not felt comfortable slipping into my pajamas with the threat of the impending storm hanging over our heads. Instead, I dressed in a comfortable pair of jeans and a warm sweatshirt.

I was glad for the extra covers I had been supplied with; it was cold down here in the cellar. All the anxiety in the room made it hard for me to fall asleep. I ended up meditating instead until finally, I slipped into a dreamless slumber.

It must have been around 6 AM the next morning, our eight day on the island, when the gale finally reached us. The entire building shuddered when that first ferocious gust of wind hit. The sound of groaning timbers and glass breaking was almost deafening, and we could smell the moisture from the pounding rain even down here in the cellar!

All of us were instantly awake. There was no way to sleep through the ruckus that ensued. Was I glad not to be anywhere upstairs at that moment! I assumed that every single window facing into the wind had been broken by that first blast! We could have been killed had it not been for the seeress' timely warning!

✦✧❀✧✦

The storm raged for hours. It was raining so hard that water was rushing down the basement stairs! Now I understood why we had all been settled at the far wall. This area was slightly higher, and we stayed dry even as other parts of the cellar were flooding.

When the water became too deep and threatened to reach our sleeping areas, a generator was put into action, and the pumps turned on. Before long, the encroaching liquid had been sent down into the sewer system.

Being curious as always, I had managed to take a peek into some of the closed-off rooms. I soon discovered that this was where all the technology was hidden. They even had internet, computers, as well as radios!

No wonder Allan had been so surprised! He had been checking the weather, and that storm had not been in the forecast!

⁂

While the tempest raged around us, I sat huddled under my covers a good part of the time to stay warm or kept company with Richard. Marie joined us whenever she could. The noise from the storm was almost deafening, even down here. Loud crashes could be heard every few minutes, and the roar of the wind sounded like jet engines.

All of a sudden, it must have been around noon, an eerie calm fell over the island. Some of us, including Richard and me, rushed up the stairs, hoping that the gale had blown itself out. Making our way carefully over the shattered glass and broken furniture, we finally made it outside.

⁂

To say that the sight awaiting us was beyond eerie is putting it mildly. We were standing in dead calm, in bright sunshine, but all around us loomed dark, greenish cloudbanks lit up by lightning and reaching far into the angry-looking sky. Those furiously swirling walls seemed pretty threatening to me!

We were in the middle of what looked like a vast funnel cloud! This must be what standing in the center of a tornado must feel like! And, to our dismay, the far wall was rapidly moving towards us!

It took us only a moment to realize the danger. All of us raced back to the basement as quickly as we could. We had barely reached the stairs when the manor started to creak from the onslaught of the next volley of violent winds.

As we ran below, we could hear the windows on the other side of the building shatter. We had been in the eye of the storm for just those brief moments! Now we were back under assault, and usually, the far side of a gale was even worse!

The tempest raged on ferociously for several more hours, but by late afternoon, the roaring sound of the wind and rain finally began to decrease. Within an hour, all the noise faded away into silence. This time, only one person was allowed to go up and check. He brought back great news. It was finally over!

Cleanup commenced almost immediately. Everyone pitched in, and within the hour, the lobby was cleared enough to make getting in and out of the manor easier. Our rooms were a totally different story.

The worst damage had been done to our living area and Richard's room. My own bedroom had south-facing windows and had escaped some of the harm but was still far from safe for occupancy. All the suites on the east and west sides were utterly uninhabitable.

The stable had fared better than the hotel as had some of the other outbuildings. They had been sheltered from the worst of the ferocious winds by the large manor house and the hills in the center of the island. A couple of the horses had sustained some minor injuries, but most were now happily grazing in the pasture.

For us humans, there was no alternative. For now, we would have to remain in the basement!

Chapter 11

The Wolf

My brother and I worked right along with the other residents of the island. Slowly but surely, the debris was being sorted. All the things too damaged to repair were thrown into the huge bonfire that had been lit in the courtyard. It was really heartbreaking to see so much of the exquisite furnishings reduced to kindling!

By the time the sun set late that evening, with all of us helping, we had made good progress. A lot of the broken windows had been boarded up, and Richard and I figured that aid from the mainland would arrive within the next couple of days.

I was tired. It had been a long day, and we had worked hard once the storm had moved on. I had already brushed my teeth and washed and was comfortably sitting on my mattress with my back to the cold stone wall. The last thing I was expecting was anyone coming through my space this late in the evening.

A guy I had never seen before suddenly parted my curtain. The movement instantly attracted my attention, and I briefly made eye contact with the man. I took in the arrogant lift of his perfectly shaped chin, the thin, cruel mouth, the straight aquiline nose, the cold look he gave me. My dislike was instant! Now that was something that did not happen very often!

For an instance, just before the curtain fell closed again, I noticed another person next to him. As I was watching, that man's features began to elongate, and he began to change. I could barely believe my eyes, but he seemed to shrink down into a wolf!

This was impossible! Shapeshifters were legend, not reality. I must have been mistaken and could not have seen what I thought I had! The partition had fallen closed and cut off my view before the transformation was complete. For a second, I wondered, was I losing my mind? Was I hallucinating?

A couple of minutes later, the first man stepped through the curtain. He had not even bothered to ask if he could enter my space. To my even greater annoyance, he rudely stepped on my bed! This guy had no manners at all, not even a little bit! What a jerk! I disliked him even further.

Everyone at the resort had been professional and polite at all times. We had been treated cordially and with respect until this guy came along. He looked sort of official, and I speculated on who he might be and what he was doing. One thing was certain, he was an unpleasant and discourteous chap!

How dare he stomp through my cubicle and on my bed without asking if he could enter! He never even said hello! There had been no acknowledgment of my presence of any kind. To say I was angry, was putting it mildly. I watched him through narrowed eyes until I noticed the huge wolf following slowly behind him.

The moment I laid eyes on the large animal; the man was completely forgotten. So, I had seen him shift after all! And, I was not crazy! Now, this was more than a little interesting! Matter of fact, I was totally fascinated and absolutely thrilled to be in the presence of something that I had thought existed only in fables!

"Come along, you! I don't have all day! Keep up!" snapped the rude chap at the hesitating creature. His nasal, unpleasant voice reminded me of his existence, and I threw the disagreeable person a venomous glare before returning to my contemplation of the wolf.

At least the animal was showing some respect for my space! Carefully skirting the bed while giving me a look that seemed to be filled with apology, the wolf slowly worked his way around my cubicle. I had no idea if all lupines were this large, but this one was huge!

 ❦

My curiosity at this point was increasing by the second. The looks I had gotten from the creature were very unusual behavior for an animal. There was an intelligence in those keen eyes that further confirmed my suspicion that all was not as it seemed and that this was truly something I had never encountered before.

Did shifters maintain their human traits when in other forms? Watching the wolf, I was starting to think so. This guy, unlike Mister Arrogance over there, must actually be a rather nice individual. My gut told me that I would have genuinely liked him.

 ❦

As a medium, I fully believe that there is much more happening around us than we are aware of. Just because we have not encountered something before, does not mean that it does not exist! Were there more people like this wolfman? I had so many questions!

Therefore, I watched the pair carefully. The man was waiting impatiently just inside the blanket screen as the large animal made its way over to him. Finally, they left my space. I assumed they were heading towards the exit just a little distance from my cozy cubicle.

When the far curtain fell closed behind the lupine, I quickly slid out from beneath the covers. There was a chance that they would come back this way, and I wanted to be ready. I was determined to take a closer look at that wolf!

As I sat there quietly, waiting, I heard footsteps return. I had guessed correctly! They were coming back in this direction! Not only was I going to force that nasty chap to move around my bed or right through it, but more importantly, my position would place me in the immediate path of the animal which would most likely go out of its way to skirt the mattress again.

Within a few moments, the unpleasant guy pushed the makeshift curtains apart. He noticed my change in position and stopped. I rose and gave him a challenging glare. The days I let any man intimidate me were long over! I was determined to stand my ground.

"Oh, for crying out loud! I need to get through, and you, you are in my way! What are you doing, defending your territory? Give me a break!" he spat before trampling straight across the upper area of my bed where a corner of the blankets had been folded down. He was leaving dirty footprints on the clean sheets! Now, I was really ticked off. What a complete ass!

The lupine once again hesitated and then slowly approached me. It was obvious that he had been made uncomfortable by the incident. The wolf had no intention of crossing over my bed like the exceedingly rude man had done. I smiled at him encouragingly and stepped aside a little to give him more space.

Finally, the huge creature came closer to me. He was even bigger than I had thought, reaching well up to my chest, and I am not a small person! And, he was absolutely magnificent!

His coat was so soft and silky that it shone even in the dim light, his back and the upper parts of his face were darker with very slight reddish hints here and there in his otherwise silvery fur. I noticed that the wolf's intelligent gaze was watching me with curiosity.

I gave him a little more room to make it easier for the animal to pass by me, but at that moment, Mr. Impatient spoke out again. "For crying out loud! She won't bite you! Come along this very minute!" A sneer distorted the haughty features.

Boy, I really did not like this guy! It felt like my hackles were rising. To my amazement, I observed the same reaction in the wolf! The back of his mane was standing almost straight up! How was this possible? Was I sensing what he was feeling or the other way around? Was there some sort of a connection between us?

I felt not the slightest bit of fear, and all my attention was on the lupine. How dare that jerk talk to this magnificent being like this? Especially since he was also a human?

I was so angry that something snapped inside me. Yes, this creature was larger than any predator I had ever been this close to, but he seemed gentle and almost kind, definitely nicer than the impatient man!

Before I knew it, I wrapped my arms around the wolf's neck. The gesture surprised me! I have no idea where I found the courage to reach out like that! I would have never even considered throwing my arms around a strange man's body and usually have even more caution with wild things!

"Don't let him bully you! You are gorgeous, as a man as well as a beast!" I whispered into his ear.

The wolf stood perfectly still for a minute then carefully turned his head so that he could meet my eyes. The second our gazes connected; an almost electric shock passed between us. He seemed as surprised as I was by the intensity of that instantaneous recognition.

At that very moment, I became aware that my entire future had been shifted, maybe even before my meeting with my new acquaintance. Some sort of bond had snapped into place, but I had no idea what it could be!

My giant new friend and I stayed staring at each other for a few seconds longer. Then, with such tenderness that it brought tears to my eyes; he laid his head against mine. For the two of us, time stopped, and the rest of the world was forgotten.

Not even Mr. Impatience seemed to dare to interrupt our silent communion. When I finally glanced up, I saw him watching us with something that could only be described as awe. Now that surprised me! Maybe this guy was not all bad, after all!

Even the most magical of moments must come to an end. We backed up a little and regarded each other with interest. I could tell that we both felt an immense sense of wonder.

Reaching out, I gently brushed down the wolf's still slightly raised hackles. I loved the feel of his soft fur under my hands. On the spur of the moment, I stepped closer and laid my head on his broad back.

The feeling of peace which enveloped me was beyond anything I had ever experienced. I could have stayed like that forever. Closing my eyes, I soaked up the strength and power emanating from him. But, I knew that he needed to go and that keeping him here with me was not really an option.

My beautiful wolf was, after all, also a man, one to whom I had not even been introduced and of whom I had only caught one brief glimpse! Tightening my arms around him, I gave him just one more brief hug. Then, reluctantly, I took a step back.

The moment I broke contact with him, it felt like the light had been doused in my world. I could see an expression of loss cross his features, and I was sure that a similar one had just flitted across my face as well.

Something appeared to draw us together, and with every step he took away from me, the ache in my heart seemed to increase. What had just happened?

Chapter 12

Magic

It took me a long time to go to sleep that night. I kept replaying the incredible scene in my mind. Something had happened between me and the wolfman that I could not explain. The other thing I was puzzling over was the alteration of my future I had sensed at that moment.

Try as I might, I could find no rational explanation for any of this. Somehow, the shifter and I had bonded, that I knew for sure. When, how, and where I had no idea. Where this would lead or what it meant for my life, I could not even imagine.

Another issue was weighing heavily on my mind. What had happened to my dream man? I had not seen him since before the storm! He had not joined me that first night in the basement, and I felt his loss even now. Where did he fit in in all this? Was he still going to enter my life?

I finally gave up trying to make sense of it all. I did not have all the facts, and I figured that time would tell what would come of this. I just had to be patient, detach from wanting to know the outcome, and let the story unfold. Not easy for someone who likes knowing her future!

Settling myself more comfortably under the covers, I started my meditation. Every so often, my mind sneaked back to that incredible scene and the sense of loss I was feeling for both men. Eventually, I fell into a deep dreamless sleep.

⋅⋅⋆⋇⟡⋇⋆⋅⋅

When I awoke the next morning, my first thought was of the wolf. The incident with the huge animal once again started playing in my mind. Try as I might, I could make no more sense of the event or the feelings it had triggered in the light of day than I had in the dead of night.

My conclusion was that something momentous had transpired, something much bigger than I had first realized. But, I had no clue what exactly had happened, not even an inkling.

I was sure that it would become apparent with time, but the not knowing really bothered me. I usually have enough premonitions to have a very good idea of what is coming my way.

Then, it occurred to me that once again, I had not seen my nighttime adventure companion. Matter of fact, I had not dreamt at all, which was very unusual for me. Had one bond been broken to be replaced with another?

Yet more questions I did not have an answer to! It was ridiculous, but instead of just missing the one, I was now missing two men!

⋅⋅⋆⋇⟡⋇⋆⋅⋅

I was so preoccupied with my thoughts that I never noticed just how quiet it was down there in that cellar. Deep in contemplation, I headed for the washroom and the toilet. I met no one on the way, but this never even registered.

All I kept thinking off was the scene of the evening before, the soft feel of the wolf's fur, his intelligent and kind eyes, and the glimpse I had caught of the gorgeous man before he had changed into a lupine. Had it all been real, or was it just a figment of my imagination? Somehow I was suddenly pretty confident that I would find out soon enough.

As I was washing my hands, I noticed that something had changed. The very faint band around my ring finger that had been there ever since my dream some months ago had darkened considerably. It was now clearly visible, almost like a tattoo. There was no longer any possibility of hiding the mark. Interesting! As if a connection had been strengthened!

But who had I further bonded with? The wolfman or my dream lover?

⁘⁘⁘

After getting ready for the day, our ninth on the island, I went looking for my brother. He was reading a book, comfortably ensconced on his bed. Together we ascended the stairs. Without an inkling what lay beyond, we pushed open the door to the lobby. Both of us came to a dead stop and gasped. My mouth must have hung open in astonishment. Richard's sure did!

The completely destroyed grand entrance, the broken windows, the demolished furniture, the shattered doors, and the shredded paintings had been completely restored! It was as if the storm had never happened! Had we been dreaming?

Neither my brother nor I could believe our eyes. We looked at each other helplessly. Just then, Marie came down the grand staircase. Seeing our confused expressions, she dropped the towels she had been carrying on one of the end tables and rushed over to us.

Grabbing our hands, she drew our attention to her. "Good morning, Richard, good morning, Ella! I know that this must seem very confusing. And, no, you are not seeing things, and the storm did happen!" she explained.

"All this is possible due to this island being a special place! I understand that it is surprising and unbelievable, but as you can see, this island has the power to heal itself! And, that's what it did!" she told us in an attempt to reassure us.

Both of us looked at her, stunned. "Relax, you two!" Marie said with a smile. "Come on, we can talk over breakfast!" She started pulling us towards the dining room, impatiently. Richard and I were too shocked to do anything but allow her to tug us along.

Breakfast was sumptuous, as always. Today, Jeffrey brought me a Caramel Macchiato, and the gluten-free rolls were right out of the oven and steamed as I cut them open. With it came raspberry and sherry jam, my absolute favorites.

This was all heavenly, but a feeling of unreality persisted. What exactly had happened? Had we imagined the storm? How could an entire island heal itself and undo such catastrophic damage? How was that even possible?

First, the changes in the catalog, then that odd storm, the wolfman, and now the complete restoration of the entire island. That there was more going on here than I had suspected was now abundantly clear!

Once I had some coffee in me, it was time to ask Marie some pointed questions. Richard was by now so in love with the woman that he would take anything she said at face value, but not me. I wanted answers and honest ones at that! I would be observing her closely to make sure that what she told us was true.

"Marie, could you please explain to us what happened here? How could everything go back to normal overnight? Was it all just a hallucination?" I queried her, watching her intensely.

"The storm was real, and so was everything you experienced, but this place is unlike any other. Did you not have scratches all over your hands last night from helping with the cleanup? Look at them now!" she answered.

Surprised, I looked at my hands. I had never even noticed that they were completely healed! The skin was supple and smooth, and all the cuts I had gotten while hauling broken bits out to the fire had completely vanished!

"Wow! I cannot believe it! This island truly is magic! No wonder I feel so drawn here!" I exclaimed.

My instinct told me that Marie was telling the truth and that everything we had experienced had been real. What a remarkable place! Who would have believed that anything like this could even be possible!

I would truly hate leaving here. My sense of wellbeing had steadily increased since setting foot on the island. I had also noticed that Richard looked healthier as well. And, he looked younger, his skin smoother. As did mine, I suddenly realized.

I was stunned. Could it be that this place had been healing and rejuvenating us all along?

⚜

Since the sun was shining brightly outside and it was a magnificent day, Marie suggested that we go kayaking or sailing. She herself intended to do some windsurfing on the far side of the island where the wind usually whipped through the channel even on balmy days.

Richard actually decided to join her! I could not believe it! The man whom I could barely get into a small sailboat was going to try standing on just a board with a sail. Boy, did he have it bad!

Suddenly, his face fell, and he looked at me. "Will you be ok kayaking on your own? I know we came here to do things together, and here I am running off on you!"

"Brother dear, I will be fine! I have been out on the Sound by myself more times than I can count. I will be extra careful to make sure that I do not get myself into trouble. You go enjoy yourself! I don't mind some alone time!" I assured him with a smile.

Richard's entire face lit up now that he was free to go spend time with his new lady love. It did my heart good to see him so happy!

Jeffrey insisted on getting the kayak ready for me and on pushing me off. I decided to let him. This was something I could have easily done on my own, but he was so very eager! I guess it was part of his duties. Along with being a waiter, he was to look after the guests.

As I paddled out of the small bay, I just happened to turn around and glance back. There was Jeffrey, still at the beach, readying a second kayak. Now this was interesting!

We were the only guests at the resort, so who was this craft being prepared for? Himself? Did he have orders to keep an eye on me and watch over me like the man up on the rock had done?

I decided to act like I was continuing on my way out of the bay by keeping up my paddling motion. I was, however, just lightly dipping the blades into the water, just enough to keep me in place.

Pretending to look for something in my pack, I surreptitiously peeked back. Sure enough, another man had joined our waiter, and they were now dragging the kayak into the water.

Was this the same man who had followed me the night before the storm? Judging from his built and graceful movements, he very well could be.

I am a good judge of character. If Jeffrey knew him and was helping him to shadow me, then I was sure that I was safe.

Chapter 13

An Unexpected Encounter

The waves were still a little choppy after yesterday's storm, but I was loving every minute of my paddling. As my craft slid silently through the water, I felt so in tune with the world around me. Never did I feel quite as alive than out kayaking or sailing. Dancing was a close second, but the sea was in my blood.

While writing was my bliss and fed my heart and soul, being out here was pure pleasure. I truly did not mind being all alone. The solitude allowed me to commune with nature and to observe the world around me without the distraction of another person's presence.

A sea lion surfaced just a few feet from me, and we silently regarded each other. Seals always reminded me of my little dog, Micha. I believe that he feels a kinship with them as well, and maybe he even realizes that they do look a little like him. He seems attracted to them.

An Unexpected Encounter

Once, while out sailing, my beloved companion took a dive overboard, wanting to go visit his cousins sunning themselves on a dock. When he hit the freezing cold water, he quickly changed his mind! He was very happy when we fished him back out of the harbor.

⁘

The only thing that could have made my stay here more perfect would have been the presence of my pets. We were a pack and did not like being separated, even when it was unavoidable at times! Whenever I was away, I missed them immensely.

As if called by my longing for my furry friends, suddenly, a big black and white head surfaced just a few feet away from me. This jolted me out of my thoughts very quickly. An orca! What a beautiful creature!

I had never been this close to one of the large animals. Curiously, we examined each other. I barely dared breathe since I was afraid to chase the magnificent being away. I have always felt a kinship to orcas and was absolutely delighted to be this near one but also a little apprehensive. If I frightened the big killer whale, it would be just too easy for it to tip over my kayak!

As I was watching, the animal drifted closer until it was right next to my craft. How incredibly magical! Did I dare touch it? It sure was worth a try! Gingerly, I reached out my hand and started to caress the large snout. This seemed to please the orca immensely. When I was rubbing just the right spot, it closed its eyes in ecstasy!

I don't know how long we drifted like this with me petting the large mammal. It ended up gently resting its big head on my kayak. What would it be like to swim with my new friend? I could not help but wonder! Flying through the water, so free and right next to such a glorious creature, must be pure heaven!

Would the orca be game? Maybe there was a wet suit I could borrow? I now regretted leaving my own at home but felt pretty confident that the resort would be able to accommodate me. I decided that I would wear a dive suit the next time I went out. That way, if I ran into my new friend again, I might just give swimming with it a try. Maybe it would even allow me to ride it!

꙳ꙫ꙳

I had been so completely absorbed in my encounter with the orca that I had paid no attention to the fact that we were drifting and that the current had captured my kayak. All of a sudden, I realized that I was much further out in the channel than I was comfortable with. As I watched in alarm, I noticed that the tide was whipping through here at an ever-increasing rate.

Oh boy! This was not good! My inattention had gotten me in serious trouble! I had almost automatically continued stroking my large friend, but now the current began to pull us apart. The distance between us increased to several feet in just a few seconds!

Panicked, I turned the kayak back towards the shore and started to paddle. But, this only made things worse! I was now broadside to the river raging through there, giving it even more purchase on my small craft! As a result, I was sliding sideways faster than I was able to make headway!

Suddenly, I felt a shove from behind that actually moved me in the direction I was trying to go. I looked back in surprise. The orca was pushing me! A wave of relief flooded through me, and I started paddling with renewed vigor. Between the large mammal and I, we were finally making some progress!

꙳ꙫ꙳

Once the strength of the current let up a little and I was no longer in such imminent danger, I noticed that the other kayak was frantically making its way towards me. It seemed that all the subterfuge was forgotten. I could not believe it, but my shadow was coming to my assistance! There was just one problem. If he came out any further, we would both be in trouble!

Using my paddle, I signaled the man to go back. After a moment's hesitation, he finally did. Good! At least I did not have to worry about him! Getting myself into a pinch due to my inattention was one thing, but dragging another person in with me was just plain unacceptable!

With the orca's help, I made it out of the current and close to the side of the island. My would-be rescuer had retreated just far enough to ensure that I could not recognize him. I waved to the man gratefully, and, after a moment's hesitation, he waved back.

✦✧❀✧✦

A bump against the side of my craft refocused my attention. The man who had held my interest but a second ago was instantly forgotten. My large friend seemed to want some more attention. I guess it was looking for a reward for saving my hide. I was only too happy to oblige. Who knows where I would have ended up had it not been for this wonderful creature?

For a few minutes, the orca once again rested its head on the kayak. It was just within easy reach, and I was thrilled to be allowed to caress it some more. This was a dream come true, and the draw I had always felt for these intelligent beings intensified even further. I had gotten a taste of something truly magical, and now, I wanted more!

As I was enjoying the interaction, I suddenly had a distinct impression that this was a male and that he was lonely. It seemed that our adventure together had created a deeper connection. My heart went out to him, and I sent him my love. In response, he slid further back on my craft, moving even closer to me.

He had been very careful not to upset the kayak, and I was astonished at his grace and circumspection. The orca could have easily tipped me over and dumped me into the frigid water during that surprising maneuver! Now, only inches separated my body from his. My new friend's eyes were closed as I gently rubbed my hands along his black and white face.

This time, however, we were both paying attention. The orca had positioned himself between me and the channel, making sure that I was not drifting back out. I was also keeping a close eye on things since I was in no mood for a repetition of that earlier experience!

Once my gentle friend had enough of the pettings, he moved back just a little from my craft. For a couple of minutes, he observed me keenly with those intelligent eyes.

I sat perfectly still as he approached once again. My encounter with him was a dream come true, and I was utterly fascinated by this handsome creature. I was also curious what he would do next. The feeling of love flowing back and forth between us was just incredible.

This time, instead of placing his head on the kayak, the orca slowly moved his big nose towards me. I was mesmerized! Closer and closer did that large mouth, thankfully closed and as I well knew, hiding many sharp teeth, progress towards my face. I was sure that he had no intention of hurting me, but still, this was just a little bit scary!

To my utter astonishment, the clever mammal placed what I could only call a gentle kiss on my cheek before sliding back and disappearing beneath the undulating waves with just the smallest of ripples!

I was in total awe, and my hand flew to cover the place the orca had touched. I could still barely believe it! What an adventure this had been! I was absolutely certain that this was one event I would never forget! I would cherish this unexpected encounter for the rest of my days!

As if emerging from a dream, I looked around. There, still keeping an eye on me, was the man with the kayak. The least I could do was try to thank him for his attempted rescue even if we would have just ended up caught in the current together. I appreciated the thought since it would have been far less scary to have someone else along on such an uncontrollable ride!

Determinedly, I struck out towards him. It took him a moment to divine my intention, which gave me the opportunity to get closer. I actually managed to get near enough to see him more clearly. I could almost recognize him. Somehow, he seemed very familiar! Was he the same man who had turned into a wolf?

Before I could positively identify him, my shadow whipped his kayak around and, with powerful strokes, sent it flying in the opposite direction. He disappeared out of sight around a grouping of rocks. What was that all about?

One thing was for sure, I was not about to chase him!

The rumbling of my stomach reminded me that it was time to head in for lunch. I had no idea how long I had been out there, but I was definitely hungry by now. I must be at least noon!

Taking one last look at the spot where the orca had disappeared, and at the rocks the man had vanished behind; I struck out towards the shore.

Chapter 14

Increased Excitement

When I got closer to shore, I noticed that Jeffrey was at the beach waiting for me. Now, this I had not expected. I would have had no problem taking care of the kayak by myself, it was not really that heavy. The young man, however, insisted that this was part of his job.

After some initial protest from my young friend, we agreed that I would help carry the slender craft up to the shed. After he washed the kayak down, we lifted it up into the cradle of the rack attached to the side of the small structure. Together, we walked back to the resort.

The waiter was usually exceedingly calm, but not today. Every cell of him seemed to vibrate with suppressed anticipation and nervous energy. What was that all about? Finally, I decided to ask him. "Jeffrey, you seem very excited today. Any special reason?"

At first, I thought he was not going to answer me, but then Jeffrey gave me a look of such innocence that I was instantly suspicious. A lie or omission was about to follow for sure! "Every month, we have a festival on this island to celebrate the full moon. Tonight is it! We always have such fun!"

"A full moon festival? That sounds amazing! Would you please tell me about it?" I enquired curiously.

"We have a bonfire, dancing, and singing of some of the old songs. We usually light the fire just before the sun sets. I bet you and your brother will just love it! All of us are looking forward to it!" the waiter explained.

Well, that did sound delightful! Richard would have a fabulous time dancing with Marie, of that I was sure! Why then was I getting the feeling that Jeffrey was hiding something important from me? His explanation had the ring of truth to it, but I was sure that something had been omitted.

⁌ↆ⁍

Richard and Marie were already in the dining room when I arrived after a quick change of clothes in my room. They were talking animatedly and seemed utterly oblivious to everything and anything around them.

Both looked flushed from the sun. Or, could it be from just a little bit more? I had noticed that things between these two were proceeding rather quickly.

For a moment, I paused in the doorway to observe them. I had never seen my brother so relaxed around any woman. It was obvious that he adored Marie and she him. If anyone deserved a good woman, it was Richard!

One day soon, it would be my turn. If the man who was destined to walk beside me had only about 90% of my brother's outstanding qualities, I would be a very fortunate woman!

⁌ↆ⁍

I tend to wear shoes that allow me to move comfortably as well as quietly. Therefore, as of yet, no one had noticed my arrival. As I stood there curiously observing the room,

I caught sight of Jeffrey's animated exchange with the rest of the staff.

It seemed that he was not the only one acting different today. The usually reserved Allan was gesturing excitedly, and George had a huge smile on his face. While the small group was talking, they kept shooting surreptitious glances at our table. They appeared to be waiting for something or someone. Me?

Well, I was more than ready to eat. I figured that I might as well make my way to the table. Out of the corner of my eye, I kept a watch on the hotel employees. Had the anticipation in the room just gone up a notch? It sure seemed so!

⚜

Usually, Jeffrey was our only waiter, but today, more of the staff kept bringing things we really did not need to the table. Every few minutes, someone would show up to inquire if we wanted anything else. What was going on here?

Richard was so focused on Marie that he was oblivious to the goings-on around us. Not that I could blame him. The lady was beautiful with her delicate features and long black hair. She was talented and smart and obviously liked my brother just as much as he liked her!

Marie had to work in the afternoon, so my brother and I decided that we would go for a hike. To my surprise, Richard had actually genuinely enjoyed his windsailing lesson, but both of us had enough of water sports for the day.

Taking something to drink and a snack along, we struck out towards the east side of the island where most of the homes were located. While we were walking, my brother was telling me all about his morning with Marie. I loved observing how animated he had become. Was being in love doing this to him, or was it the magic? Or, maybe a little of both?

⚜

The center of the island was covered with evergreen trees climbing up the slope of a small mountain. The woods were interspersed in the lower areas with wide-open fields of tall golden grass, and the path led us past a serene little lake. I was instantly charmed. The more I saw of the place, the deeper I fell in love with this isle.

Richard and I had not been to the village before. I suggested that we hike in that direction because I wanted to check out the homes. Jeffrey had mentioned that a couple houses were up for sale, and, at this point, I was more than a little interested.

The charming island was roughly divided into two sections. The resort and another gorgeous large house took up the west side, the other inhabitants had their homes on the eastern half in what was almost a small town of around 13 homes.

Winters can be harsh out here with violent gales and ice-cold winds streaming of the frigid water. Days then are short, and darkness falls early. Having the houses close together means that it is easier to keep track and aid one another if the need ever arises. Plus, pleasant company on those dreary evenings helps to keep the blues away.

Building small enclaves instead of spread-out subdivisions made a lot of sense to me. Where I live, each of us has several acres. This suits me most days but can get lonely.

Being left to my own devices, I tend to dive into creating, especially whenever I have a new story to tell. I am very comfortable with my own company, and as a writer, I tend to escape into my fantasy world.

All that being said, I would still prefer having a special someone or at least close by neighbors around. In my opinion, life is just so much more fun shared!

⁘⁘⁘⁘

As we were hiking towards the hamlet, I once again felt watched. I was sure that we were being followed, most likely by the same man who seemed to be keeping an eye on me. Maybe those times my brother and I had felt scrutinized, he had also been tagging along!

I decided not to mention this to Richard, he was enjoying himself, and the last thing I wanted to do was to spoil his good mood. Before too much longer, we reached the collection of homes. My brother really liked one of the available houses, and I was surprised when he started talking about wanting to buy it.

The island was an isolated place and more conducive to my business than his! Marie must have made even more of an impression on him than I had first thought! I could not help but smile as we started walking back.

Now that I knew he was there, I kept catching flashes of my shadow. Since he was so good at camouflage, I was certain that he was allowing me to see him. In a way, there was a feeling of security in knowing that he was following us. If Richard and I ran into trouble, he would be on hand to lend assistance.

As we were hiking along, I was drinking in the beauty around us. I never got tired of the contrast of the dark fir trees against that blue, blue sky lit up by sunshine, the bright green moss on the rocks, and the silvery spots of lichens splattered here and there.

The Pacific Northwest is one of the most magical places I have ever been to, especially in the summertime. I have been in love with the area ever since the very first time I traveled there so many years ago.

Being fully present in the moment, observing all that was around me, and being grateful for the beauty I saw was my way of getting out of any funk. Not that I was feeling out of sorts this day, no, just the opposite. Now that I was paying attention, I realized that my stomach was actually fluttering with excitement.

What was all that about? Thoughtfully, I investigated the feeling further and discovered an intense sense of positive anticipation. Interesting! So, the staff members were not the only ones looking forward to something amazing today! I just wished that I had a clue what was coming my way!

⸙

Our walk back was quiet and uneventful. Both Richard and I were deeply in thought. I suddenly realized that I had not shared my experience with the Orca. Nor had I told him about my dreams or some of the other events which had taken place while I was off on my own. When had I become so secretive? I usually told most things to my brother!

I could not bring myself to disrupt the tranquility of the serene woods around us. This just did not feel like the right moment for catching up. Therefore, Richard and I walked on in peaceful silence.

By the time we made it back to the manor, it was time for dinner. As we passed through the courtyard, we could see the large pile of wood that had been stacked up for the bonfire later that night. The staff had certainly been busy in our absence!

A smiling Marie met us at the door. After an affectionate greeting, she informed us that the meal was almost ready. Richard and I rushed to our rooms for a quick wash and a change of clothes. Then, we headed down to the dining hall to eat. We were both looking forward to the evening.

⸙

The rosemary chicken the cook had prepared this night was superbly seasoned and the vegetables crisp and flavorful. For some reason, I was too excited to truly do this superb meal justice. My stomach was tight and fluttery, and I decided to stick to water instead of my usual small glass of wine.

After dinner, we were served pecan shortbread cookies for dessert along with a bowl of homemade vanilla ice-cream. With whipped cream, naturally! Now, this was too good not to savor, and I ended up genuinely enjoying the delightful treat. Good thing that I was getting plenty of exercise!

The closer it got to nighttime, the more the sense of excitement grew noticeable in the air. Something was about to happen, I just knew it, but I did not have the slightest clue what! That was very unusual for me, and I was not sure I liked it!

Finally, the sun was starting to go down, and it was time to head outside and watch the fire being lit. A three-man band set up and started the entertainment. They played fiddle and bagpipes, a magical mix. I was impressed, these guys were good, and I loved the songs.

The rousing music worked its way into my blood. Soon we were all dancing, and it did not take long before I totally lost track of Richard and Marie.

Chapter 15

A Nightly Visitor

It was getting late, and the full moon celebration was still in full swing. We were all having a fabulous time. I had been dancing almost nonstop for the last couple of hours. In passing, I caught an occasional glimpse of Richard and Marie who seemed to be genuinely enjoying themselves.

In the last few minutes, the fire had started to collapse in on itself. With one final tune and a whirl around the flames, the festivities came to an end. When the music stopped, I stood there panting. The rhythm of the last song had been intricate and fast, and I had happily risen to the challenge of keeping time with the beat.

The dancers started saying goodnight and heading off into the dark. Soon only Richard, I, and the staff of the hotel remained. I was still feeling kind of wired, but it was just about midnight and time to head to bed.

Our suite had been fully restored to its previous glory, and all my things placed back in their proper places. Richard and I said goodnight to each other in the living area and headed for our separate rooms.

To my astonishment, candles had been set up all over my chamber, and a sort of path created with lights and pink rose petals that lead straight to the bathroom. Curiously I followed the fragrant surprise into the bath. The scent filling the room was amazing, and rose petals had been strewn all over the freshly filled tub and the adjacent floor.

My jaw dropped. This was magnificent and completely unexpected. How sweet of the staff to anticipate my needs and go out of their way to make this night truly memorable. Gratefully I sunk into the pleasantly warm water.

I was blissfully soaking in the large tub when Marie soundlessly entered the room. I was surprised that she would enter uninvited and was going to speak, but she held a finger to her lips and then pointed in the direction of Richard's room to keep me silent.

In her hands, she carried a beautiful robe, and she motioned for me to get out of the tub. My curiosity was now fully aroused, and I decided to oblige her. I truly wanted to know where all this would lead.

After drying myself off with one of the soft towels, I slipped into the dressing gown she was holding out to me. Grabbing my hand, Marie led me into my room and sat me down in front of the makeup desk. Quickly and skillfully, she highlighted my checks, added a touch of color to my eyelids and applied a light coat of mascara to my lashes. Last, she gently painted my lips with a beautiful, shimmering rose color.

Next, Marie tamed my wavy mane. My hair usually looks rather nice even left to its own devices, but she managed to curl it so that it gently framed my face. The effect was stunning! I looked like a model, my eyes wide and innocent and perfectly complimented by the soft shade of the lipstick.

Next, she drew a dress I had never seen before out of my wardrobe. The chemise was of the softest white silk, and the dark blue overdress laced up in the front. It was magnificent and right out of a medieval movie, a perfect period costume. I noticed that the embroidery was done in gold thread and that it was bordered with real pearls and sparkling gems. This must cost a fortune!

Once I had been laced into this gorgeous creation, Marie placed a wreath of small, fragrant roses onto my head. Then, she turned me so that I could look into the mirror. I almost did not recognize myself! I looked absolutely stunning, like a goddess of the full moon!

I still had no idea where we were going when Marie took my hand and led me out of the door of my bedroom. Silently, we exited the suite. The manor was deadly quiet, as if no living being resided within, as we glided down the grand staircase. The entry was wide open, and a horse-drawn carriage was waiting for us in the courtyard.

Marie still had not spoken a word, and the atmosphere around us was so filled with mystery and anticipation that it did not lend itself to asking questions. There was an expectancy in the air that filled me with excitement as well as anxiety and very efficiently kept me from speaking. Something very special was about to happen, of that I was sure!

I was facing forward in the open carriage and noticed that the track before us seemed to appear out of nowhere. When I looked back, just a few feet behind us, the trail we had been on had all but disappeared. Magic, again! As we traveled further, we swung onto an actual path. In the distance I could see a bright light. We were moving towards it. As we got closer, people started to line the ancient road.

I had guessed by now that our destination was the stone circle, and I was right. When we pulled up just outside it, Marie disembarked and held out her hand for me to come with her. Together, we walked into the circle and joined the people within.

All of a sudden, memory came flooding in. It rushed in so violently that I stumbled for a moment. I had to reach out to Marie to steady myself. The entire world was spinning around me!

Once I regained my equilibrium, I raised my head. There he was! Taren! My mate, my love! A smile which rivaled the sun lit up my face.

This was the night I would partake of the elixir that would pave the way for us to be joined forever! Happiness filled my heart and soul as Marie led me forward to place my right hand in Taren's. As my fingers neared his, a bright spark erupted between us. Now, this was something! Our mere touch was electric!

For a moment, all that existed for me in this whole world was the gorgeous man in front of me. Taren was regarding me with an awe that mirrored my own. Never before had I felt an attraction or love for anyone as strong as I felt at that instant!

Just touching him sent fire through my veins and caused heat to erupt in my loins. My body, which had been asleep and without desire for any other man during my waking hours for a while now, came alive with a vengeance. My pulse started to race and, had he been any closer, I don't think I could have caught one single breath!

With a sudden flash of foresight, I knew at that moment that life with Taren would be everything I had ever dreamed of. He would walk beside me, love me, and be my best friend. We would have a happy, lasting relationship built on mutual respect, admiration, and appreciation. And, naturally, the most amazing sexual chemistry! How could we not?

I felt so incredibly lucky and blessed that tears filled my eyes. I had finally found my true soul mate, the one I would be able to love without fear and who understood that due to my past, I needed the emotional security he was offering me.

Taren was more than willing to be my rock, my shelter from the storm, as well as my hero. With him by my side, my creativity would truly grow wings.

Wolves mate for life, and so would we.

Marie's soft voice, raised up in a jubilant song, brought us back to the moment. We were here for a reason, after all! Together we faced the makeshift altar that had been erected within the ancient stones.

The gypsy was patiently waiting for us to notice her. I realized that Angelique must also be the high priestess of this close-knit community. That lady sure wore a number of hats!

Angelique smiled at me in greeting, and I felt instantly completely at ease. With this rite, my whole life would be transformed into something magical. I was looking forward to this, welcomed the change.

I noticed the seeress' questioning look. She wanted to make sure that I was ready for this. A bright, happy smile spread over my face, and I gave her a nod. I was more than prepared to take this first step on my journey with Taren!

Matter of fact, I was eager for the ceremony to begin.

Chapter 16

Metamorphosis

On the altar in the ancient stone circle sat a goblet encrusted with rubies. It looked very old, and I had no doubt that it probably was. The priestess faced us and regarded us both solemnly for a moment. Then, commandingly, she reached out towards us. Taren and I obeyed and placed our left hands in hers.

The gypsy intoned a blessing over us that the assembled group joyfully repeated. I could not stop smiling. Here, finally, was my dream come true! I was only too aware of how much I wanted this and that I was prepared to do anything necessary to secure a future with this gorgeous man.

Reverently, the priestess placed my left hand in Taren's. We were now holding both hands, virtually creating a circle and making us one. Then, Angelique stepped back and bowed in front of the altar. She approached it with obvious veneration.

After a second prayer, which was once again repeated by the others present, she deferentially reached her hands out for the cup and lifted it off the altar.

༈ ༈

I could see that the liquid contained in that goblet was steaming and had a slight glow to it. That scared me a bit for a moment. It reminded me vividly of the Addams Family and some of the brews they served their unsuspecting visitors. Could a regular human survive drinking this?

Marie smiled at me, reassuringly, and the feeling of anxiety ebbed away. I was convinced that neither Taren nor anyone else within this circle would hurt me. If drinking this strange potion was what it took to be joined with my love, so be it!

Still, my hands were shaking just a little as the priestess turned in my direction with the magic-filled cup. The ritual was about to begin, and my life would be altered forever. Once I drank this mysterious liquid, there would be no going back!

༈ ༈

Angelique ceremoniously advanced towards me and came to a stop in front of me with the ancient goblet. Taren released my left hand and took a small step back. Here we go, I could not help thinking.

"Are you willing to join this man, Taren, he who is both, man and wolf? To become his mate, to run at his side, from this day forward?" she asked.

"Yes, I am!" I answered loud and clear without a moment's hesitation.

"Are you willing to partake of this magic elixir to become one of us?" came the second question.

I looked the gypsy straight in the face. I was not totally certain what exactly would happen to me once I drank that brew, but if it meant that I would have an actual life, not just a dream life, with Taren, I was prepared to do whatever it took.

"Yes, I am," I therefore responded and, disengaging my right hand from my future mate, reached out for the cup with both hands. I was ready and willing.

Losing that physical contact with Taren had felt like the sun had just stopped shining, but there was no way I was going to risk spilling that precious elixir, the one thing standing between me and a life of pure bliss!

⚜

The goblet felt warm in my hands, and I tentatively took the first drink. Not too bad! It could have been worse! Since I had been told that I needed to drink all of it, I figured that I might as well get it over with. Therefore, I gulped down the rest.

Angelique gently took the empty cup from my hands, and Taren stepped close and wrapped his arms around me. I could sense the expectancy in the air. All were waiting to see what would happen.

After what seemed like only a minute, a tingling began to spread through my whole body. This was followed by a strange vibration. Both sensations increased until it felt like fire was racing through my veins. Had I still held the gem covered goblet, I would have dropped it for sure!

⚜

Taren was right there to support me. Gently, he picked me up and laid me down on the altar. He stayed with me, his face just inches from mine. To make me more comfortable, he unlaced the beautiful overdress. I sighed with relief as he undid the binding. With Marie's help, he carefully stripped it away.

My love kept talking to me and made sure that our gazes stayed locked while my body was going through the change. I don't remember all of that initial transformation, but I do remember that is was fairly brutal.

There was so much excruciating pain that I saw reflected in his eyes. I think that Taren was taking some of that agony to make the metamorphosis easier for me.

Screams were echoing in my ears. Later it dawned on me that they had been my own!

I don't know how long that unspeakable torment lasted, but towards the end, it felt like my bones were breaking and reshaping themselves. When the anguish finally subsided, I could see the world much more clearly and differently somehow. Taren was standing in front of me with a delighted grin.

As I went to reach for him, I realized that I no longer had hands! I had wings! Marie brought over a mirror, and I looked at myself. I was an owl! A huge, beautiful almost pure grey owl with brilliant blue eyes! And, I was sitting in the middle of a cloud of soft silk! Now this was not something I had expected!

After the shift, much of the rest of the night was pretty much a blur. I remember a large raven patiently teaching me how to use those newly acquired wings. Boy, was I clumsy at first! It was much harder than it looked! Perfecting this new skill and being able to fly without hitting a tree or anything else took a while!

In the beginning, Taren would intercept me whenever I was about to bump into something. He would laugh and catch me in his arms. Now that part was most certainly fun and might have contributed to me not learning as fast as I could have.

Once I finally got a hang of things, I recall flying above my mate in his sleek wolf shape. We were dodging in and out of trees. I have a shadowy memory of racing together through the meadows and woods, playing chase, getting more used to my wings.

At one time, I soared up into the sky towards the moon. I was filled with a pure joy that is hard to describe. Just being able to glide like that was exhilarating! After hovering above the trees for a bit, my love got my attention and coaxed me back down to earth.

He ran, I flew, and we played, both of us filled with a sense of indescribable happiness that we were finally able to be together. After we had worn off some of that exuberance, we found a pleasant spot on some rocks overlooking the Sound and cuddled close. Now that was pure bliss!

✦✦✦

Towards morning, we returned to the circle. Taren and Marie taught me how to turn back into my human form. This was once again incredibly painful, but my love assured me that it would get easier with each shift. The first couple of times were always the worst.

The open carriage swiftly took all three of us back to the manor once we were dressed. I was incredibly tired and almost fell asleep with my head on Taren's broad shoulder.

Parting from this man whom I already loved so deeply was not something I was looking forward to, even if it was just for a little while longer. I would have adored falling asleep in the circle of his arms, loved, safe, and secure.

I knew that I would see him again in a few hours, at breakfast. Taren would be staying around the hotel from now on, and we intended to spend as much time as possible together. One of the first things we intended to do was introduce my new mate to my brother!

✦✦✦

After one final hug, Taren and I went our separate ways. Marie helped me slip back into my room. She helped me out of my beautiful dress and the silk undershirt and into my pajamas.

Then, lovingly, she covered me up and tucked me in like a child. Even so I was incredibly tired; there was one thing I just had to know.

"Marie, do you love Richard?" I could not help but ask. A soft, happy smile lit up the lady's face. It was actually all the answer I needed.

"Yes, I love him," she whispered. "Don't worry, I will never hurt him. I can promise you that. He is too special a man!" With those words, she brushed a strand of hair out of my face.

Somehow, out of their own volition, my eyes closed, and I fell deeply asleep.

Chapter 17

The Suitor

Day 10 of our stay on the island dawned bright and beautiful. I was sound asleep when the sun began to make its way up into the sky. It had been a very long night! The island, however, worked its usual magic on me, and after four hours of deep sleep, I was wide awake. I lingered for a moment, stretching and enjoying the warmth of the bed.

Poor Richard! I do hope he had gone to breakfast without me! It was already after 10 AM, and he always got up early!

He was usually at work long before I even opened my eyes. These last few days had been the exception to the rule, but meeting my dream man every night had been more intriguing than writing or reading!

Then I remembered. Last night, I had met him for real! That was enough for me to happily bounce out of bed and hurry through my morning routine. I took special care with my makeup and dress, I wanted to look beautiful just for Taren.

⛧

Richard was reading as I entered the living area. He looked up at me and smiled. Last night had been fairly late for him, but he looked well-rested. Being on the island had definitely been good for him!

Three years ago, my brother had been diagnosed with a deadly disease, and I had almost lost him. I was so grateful that his life had been spared and that he was recovering his health. I had watched him make remarkable progress in the few days since we had arrived at the resort and was absolutely thrilled that he was steadily improving.

Maybe living on this island was not such a bad idea for him after all! Especially if it meant that he could stay with Marie!

⛧

"Good morning! Did you have breakfast, or have you been waiting for me?" I asked after giving Richard a loving hug.

"I had a little something, but I am ready for more now! How about you?" came his response.

I laughed. "I seem to be starving! And, I need coffee! Shall we?"

Arm in arm, Richard and I headed for the dining room.

⛧

As soon as we entered, Marie came to greet us. I noticed immediately that our table was set for four this time. I could barely hide my pleasure at this.

"Good morning, you two! Did you sleep well?" We both nodded, and Marie continued, "Do you mind if a friend of mine joins us for breakfast?"

Richard, at all times the perfect gentleman, immediately answered, "Any friend of yours, my love, is always welcome!"

Marie smiled at my brother with such affection that my heart just melted. It was so wonderful to see him in love

~ 134 ~

and being loved! His lady was not just beautiful but honest and kind. No wonder Richard was willing to do just about anything to stay near her!

⊱✦⊰

"Good morning!" a melodic voice interrupted my contemplation, and I whipped around. There he was! The companion of my nightly adventures and last night's exhilarating race through the moonlit woods! Once again it hit me. He was just as gorgeous in real life as he had been in my dreams!

"Marie, would you please introduce us?" Taren requested quietly. His eyes were focused on me even as he was addressing his friend.

"I am so sorry!" Marie exclaimed. She had been so focused on Richard that she had never noticed Taren approach.

"Ella and Richard, may I introduce you to one of my oldest friends, Taren StClair? Taren, meet Ella and Richard Montgomery, the siblings from Seattle I have been telling you about."

Taren stepped up to me and took my left hand. Looking deep into my eyes, he turned it over and placed a gentle kiss into my palm. The gesture was so intimate it sent shivers through me. I could not tear my gaze away from his handsome face.

⊱✦⊰

In a way, we were already a couple, but we were determined that this official courtship would turn out to be a most delightfully romantic time, something we would always remember. I was looking forward to learning more about Taren, to actually spending time with him in person, and I sure hoped that he sailed!

There was so much I did not know about this amazing man, and I was genuinely going to enjoy finding out all about him. I just hoped that he and Richard would get along well. But, since they were both good, decent men, I saw no reason why they would not.

~ 135 ~

After what seemed like an eternity but had just been a few moments, Taren released my hand and reluctantly broke eye contact. I instantly missed being warmed by his gaze and his tender touch.

He turned to my brother who had been watching us closely. Richard was very perceptive, and my spellbound reaction to this gorgeous stranger and his to me had not escaped him. They shook hands, eyeing each other warily.

I was amused by their behavior. The two regarded each other for several minutes, sizing each other up, before coming to a consensus. Richard seemed to approve of this man who had shown such interest in his little sister because he smiled warmly at Taren.

One hurdle down! This courtship was going to be fun!

⚜

Today, the juice tasted even more amazing. We had been served a glass every morning since our arrival, but it had not come close to this. I could sense it making its way through my body, and it felt like it left love and laughter in its wake.

The cook had truly outdone himself as well. Instead of the usual plain roles that I just adored, he had created heart-shaped cinnamon rolls. Hmmm, interesting! When the cream in my macchiato was also in the shape of a heart, I could not help but smile. I guess love was in the air!

The four of us got on famously, which seemed to greatly please the staff. Jeffrey, our waiter, was usually pretty cheerful already but this morning, he was beaming from ear to ear. Who exactly was Taren StClair?

⚜

Breakfast turned out to be a lively affair and lasted much longer than usual. None of us seemed to be in a hurry to rush off, which suited me fine. After a while, Richard became deeply involved in a discussion with Marie which allowed Taren and me to get to know each other better.

Our eyes kept meeting, and eventually, we scooted closer together. Before long, Taren was openly holding my hand, but neither one of us actually noticed. It felt natural, and we were so preoccupied that such a show of affection just kind of happened. To finally actually be able to be in each other's presence was so amazing.

The more we talked, the more our bond strengthened. There was much that could not be said in public just yet, but our eyes communicated those things just the same. The world fell away, and there was only him and me.

"Ella? Taren? Hello! World to Ella and Taren!" The words finally broke through, and we turned to Marie and Richard who were openly laughing at us. Both of us turned red. We had completely forgotten about them!

"Why don't the four of us go for a hike? The temperature is just right, not too hot yet. Well, how about it?"

Taren and I hastily agreed. Hiking sounded great as did anything else just as long as it included being together!

Just as we were about to leave the dining room, Taren spoke up. "Would you ladies please excuse Richard and I for a moment?"

Then, turning to my brother, he asked, "Richard, may I have a word?" The two men moved aside, just out of earshot. For a moment, Marie and I exchanged a puzzled glance before watching them with curiosity.

At first, Taren spoke, and Richard listened, then they took turns. Eventually, the two smiled at each other and shook hands. What was that all about?

Marie and I were mystified. We looked at each other and shrugged. Neither one of us had a clue what the two could be discussing. I guess we would find out!

It was afternoon by the time our small group set out for the hike. Before long, we ended up pairing up. Taren and I were soon lagging behind, and Richard and Marie were too involved with each other to notice. I was delighted to watch my brother reach out and offer the lady his hand. About time he found someone to share his life!

Taren had followed my gaze, and we smiled at each other. "I am happy that you approve. Marie is an amazing lady."

"She is, isn't she? I am thrilled to see my brother with someone who seems to care as much about him as he does her! He has been through a lot and deserves some happiness. This island seems to be good for him!"

"Do you think he would be willing to live here?" Taren inquired.

"He actually likes one of the houses in the little village, so yes. I was rather surprised at first, but I am starting to believe that he would do anything to be with Marie."

Taren stopped and turned me to face him. He gently cupped my face in his hands. "I have received your brother's permission to court you. Would you please remain here with me, on this island?"

So that was what their discussion had been all about! How thoughtful of Taren to show my brother and me such respect! Not too many men nowadays had such a sense of courtesy!

⁖⁎⁘⁙⁖

Until that moment, this amazing love affair between Taren and I had felt more like a fairytale fantasy. But, him asking me in all seriousness if I would stay on the island with him brought reality crashing in. Some serious questions were suddenly burning in my mind.

I was aware that we were already bonded and in love, but how compatible were we? Would we truly be able to build a happy lasting relationship together? Did this gorgeous man share my passions in life?

"Do you like to sail?" I, therefore, asked him with all seriousness. Taren looked at me in surprise and burst out laughing.

"Yes, I actually do, and I even have a boat I think you will love," came his response.

"Are you willing to accept as well as support my writing and go on book tours with me?" came my next inquiry. This was very important to me. I had dreams and goals and see bringing the tales to the world that the Universe wants telling as my life's purpose.

"Sweetheart, anything that brings you bliss will always have my full backing. I am also willing and able to help you with the marketing if you like! I promise that you can count on me!" the amazing man replied.

"What about my pets? They are my pack, and I love them!" came my final question.

"Our pack now, my love, our pack. They are a part of your life, which makes them a part of mine." My mate assured me. How did he know just what to say?

⁘⁘⁘

On impulse, I threw my arms around Taren's neck. I placed a brief, gentle kiss on his lips before backing up a little once more. I was filled with joy and brimming with happiness. Looking deep into his warm, kind eyes, I gave him my answer.

"Then, yes! This island is beautiful, and I would love to live here with you. My pets would be very happy here, and it is a perfect place for me to write! It would be so inspiring to wake up to a view of the Sound each morning, to be so close to the water, to have these magnificent woods to hike and play in!"

"Ella, I would love to pull you close and kiss you about now, but I have promised your brother to take it slow!" Taren groaned. He was grinding his teeth in frustration.

Well, I had made no such promise now, had I? A mischievous look found its way onto my face as I stepped close and once again wrapped my arms around Taren's neck. I pulled his mouth down to mine.

⁘⁘⁘

Once again, an electric shock sparked between us, but this time, as his lips drew near mine. It surprised both of us for a moment, and we pulled back to regard each other with an immense sense of wonder. As we were looking deeply into each other's eyes, the pull became so strong that we tried it once more. And, we succeeded!

This was our very first actual kiss! The dream kisses had been nothing compared to the reality! My body melted into his, and his long fingers wrapped themselves around my waist. Desire flared brightly between us, and heat rushed through my body. I swear my toes were curling inside my shoes!

As he deepened the kiss, emotions of pure love for this gorgeous man began to overwhelm me. I thought my heart would burst. He truly was the mate I had been searching for my whole life! I was the luckiest woman alive and immense gratitude for having been granted this dream filled my entire being.

When we finally pulled apart, we were both panting. Of Richard and Marie, thankfully, nothing was to be seen. Holding hands and laughing like children, we rushed to catch up.

⁕⁕⁕

If this was what being in love truly felt like, going through all the pain to learn to love myself and to grow into the person I had become, had been more than worth it! I would have gladly suffered through all of it again just to arrive back at that moment.

Sometimes, however, even the best-laid plans do not work out. Of one thing Taren and I were now certain. We had underestimated the attraction between us and the depth of the feelings that already existed.

The slow courtship Taren and I had originally intended was not going to work!

⁕⁕⁕

Eventually, we caught up with Richard and Marie. I am not sure that they even missed us! It seemed that these two were making progress as well. Their eyes were shining, and they were all smiles as they gazed at each other. Seeing them such made me even more happy than I already was.

The trail we were following took us to the very rock where I had first noticed someone observing me. What a view! From up here, one could see the entire bay where the kayaks and sailboats were stored as well as the islands beyond! Had it been Taren who had been hiding here that day?

I stepped close, pulled his head down, and whispered in his ear. "Was it you up here keeping an eye on me?" His gentle smile told me everything I needed to know. He had been the one watching over me to make sure that I was not harmed!

I could feel it in my very gut that he would always be there to look out for me. He was the kind of man who would protect me and keep me safe, an honorable, upstanding mate, a true life-partner.

⁕

I have always sensed things or knowledge, and ideas would just pop into my head. I could feel it before someone came over and was aware of how things stood in my relationships. This instinct had served me well over the years, especially once I had come to realize the trend of my previous partners and knew intuitively whom to avoid.

Suddenly, visions of my future with Taren flooded into my mind's eye. I saw different scenes moving forward in time, and I smiled happily. We would have an amazing life together, a lasting love, a closeness few shared, wonderful adventures, and a connection so deep it would be difficult to know where I began, and he ended.

In the past, that would have terrified me but not with Taren. With him, I was willing to allow this melding of two souls.

⁕

Happy tears filled my eyes. Taren eyed me with concern. I smiled up at him, stepped closer, and laid my head on his broad chest. Being the man of honor that he is, my love hesitated for just a moment. Then, after giving my brother an apologetic look, he wrapped his strong arms around me and held me tight.

Deep peace, like I had never known before, flooded through my heart and soul. I was finally home!

Chapter 18

The Honest Truth

The emotional scene on the rock had been a dead giveaway of mine and Taren's feelings for each other. After I had regained my composure, my love and I had moved apart. I had smiled at Richard to reassure him and had settled myself comfortably on the moss-covered stone.

Seeing that I was relaxed and content to remain, the others had followed my example. The four of us stayed up there on our perch a little bit longer, enjoying the view and the sun on our faces. It was, after all, a beautiful day and a magical spot.

The conversation had been a tad halting at first but had soon picked up. Marie had told us about some of her concerts, and Richard had been only too happy to entertain us with his own experiences in the music world.

My brother is a talented pianist as well as a skilled tuner. He is always busy. His clients love him, and some of the people he has met and worked with are pretty amazing.

His intention to move to the island would upset a number of piano owners.

⚜

As was to be expected, Richard had been more than a little surprised to see how far Taren and I had progressed in our relationship in just a few hours. On the way back to the resort, my love and I decided that it was time to tell him the truth.

That evening, after yet another sumptuous dinner, the four of us sat down by the fire in the great room. It was summer, but evenings out here in the San Juans could still be rather cool. This was one of those nights when the temperature was just too low to sit outside comfortably.

As soon as the staff withdrew, Taren laid it all out for my brother. At first, his words were met with disbelief. This was too far out, to magical for Richard. He had a hard time wrapping his brain around the fact that legends might actually exist.

And, what did this mean for his budding relationship with Marie? Was she a shapeshifter as well? I could see the fear written plainly on my brother's expressive face, and so could she for she reached out and took his hands in hers.

"Richard, nothing between us will change. You can join us or not, I will still love you and live with you," she reassured him. I visibly saw my brother relax, but he still did not believe everything he had been told. He had come to accept that the island was magic, but people changing into animals? That was too far out of his comfort zone!

The three of us realized that there was only one way to convince Richard. But, should I shift or Taren? We exchanged concerned glances; words spoken aloud were no longer necessary between us. Definitely not Marie, my brother was not ready for that. My love finally decided to make the decision for us. He changed into his wolf form.

For a moment, Richard reacted with fear. He jumped up from his seat and backed away but calmed when I stepped up to the huge animal and wrapped my arms around him. Taren could not resist nuzzling me. It would be so wonderful not to have to hide the way we felt about each other any longer!

When a sense of wonder entered my brother's eyes, I knew that we had won him over. Richard turned his gaze to Marie, and she smiled at him reassuringly.

"Marie, I hope you do not mind me asking. If he is a wolf, then what are you?" Richard inquired. I was curious about that myself. I had been too busy with Taren and my own shapeshifting the night before to pay much attention to anything else.

Marie looked down shyly. "I change into a doe. I only do this on rare occasions. It is not as easy for me as it is for some of the others."

Richard returned to his seat and reached out for her hands. "Is that why it does not matter to you if I take the elixir or not?" he asked gently.

Marie looked up at him with tears in her eyes. "That and I love you."

The joy flooding across my brother's face lit up the room. He pulled Marie close to him and started kissing her. I smiled to myself and quietly left the room with the large wolf padding along beside me.

The next day, our 11th on the island, Taren and I decided to go sailing. He was looking forward to showing me his other pride and joy, his new boat. I had not seen her because she had just been delivered. This would be her maiden voyage. The vessel had been anchored on the far side of the island, but he had her brought around to the west side early that morning.

Taren took my hand and led me towards the patio. Before he would let me exit the building, he stepped behind me and covered my eyes. Thus, we moved out on the terrace, me close to his chest being steered to just the right spot for the perfect first view.

"Are you ready?" Taren whispered in my ear. I nodded, and my mate removed his hands. I was in love just as soon as I laid eyes on her. Long and sleek with clean, perfect lines, this magnificent vessel promised to be fast and fun to sail. I could still barely believe that it and this wonderful man would be part of my life from now on!

⁕⁕⁕⁕⁕

About an hour later, we were on our way out to the boat. We had packed a lunch and intended to spend the rest of the day sailing. Richard and Marie had made plans of their own. I had overheard them talking about taking a closer look at the house my brother liked so much. I had not been able to suppress the happy smile which found its way on my face at hearing those words.

The name of the boat was an additional thing I just loved about her. Taren had named her *Mermaid*, a nickname I had been given in the past. A thought occurred to me suddenly, and I started to wonder.

Would my affinity for the ocean and its creatures also allow me to change into something which would make it possible for me to swim in its depths? Somehow I thought so. That was definitely something I intended to explore!

⁕⁕⁕⁕⁕

The boat was absolutely stunning, the cabins below light and airy. The main bedroom had a comfortable queen-sized bed and actual closets as well as enough space for all the things I might want to bring with me on an extended sea voyage. This was one vessel one could really feel at home on no matter how long the trip!

What truly surprised me were the other additions. There was a perfect place for a guinea pig cage in the main cabin. It even had straps to secure it! All I would have to do is slide in the crate, latch the buckles, and my boys would be safely locked into place!

To top it all off, on each side of our bed was a comfortable place to sleep for the dogs!

⁕⁕⁕⁕⁕

I love my little pack. Being separated from them felt like part of me was absent. Exploring amazing places lost some of its allure when I was missing my furry family. But, I could not blame my love if he would prefer to leave them behind. Did Taren truly intend for them to travel with us on this brand-new vessel? I had to know!

"Taren, would you be good with the pets onboard? I know it makes things harder having to take the dogs to shore at least twice a day. And, they may scratch up your beautiful boat." I voiced with some apprehension.

Taren instantly sensed my distress. He was amazing like that, sensitive, empathetic, and compassionate. He had been at the nav station getting the boat ready to sail, but now, he rushed to my side and wrapped me in his strong arms. This was all new to me, someone actually caring to give comfort when he felt that I was upset!

"Look around you. Remember that dream you had some months ago? That night was the first meeting of our souls. I had her built after that. That space there is designed especially for a cage, and those areas over there just lack the dogs' beds. I thought that we would choose those together," he told me with a smile.

My whole world rocked. Taren had this boat build just for us? Who was this man I was tying my life to? Maybe it was time that I asked some more questions.

✦✧✦✧

Instead of sailing, we ended up talking. After a while, we brought out lunch, but there was much that needed to be said. The food remained almost untouched on the table. Taren and I were too preoccupied with each other to pay it much attention.

This was a most unusual courtship. Fate seemed to have decided to weld us together before we had even met. I needed to know where I stood, and I had many, many questions I wanted to ask.

✦✧✦✧

I wanted to know more about Taren. Who was this man that fate had bonded my soul to? He was happy to comply and told me about his family, about the love they had shared, about his happy childhood on the island filled with fun and laughter, and about the deaths of his parents and younger sister in a car accident on the way to Seattle. Their loss had affected him deeply.

As he spoke about his life, I began to understand why he treasured our relationship as much as I did. Bonding for life made the selection of the right mate so much more challenging! To be able to choose wisely, one had to first know and love the self. Taren had been searching for the soul connection we now shared for a very long time.

What amazed me was the total acceptance we had of each other. Neither one of us cared about the past; we saw it as a preparation for our life together. All that mattered was the now, the people we had become. The pain and disappointments we had both experienced allowed us to truly treasure the incredible gift of loving and being loved that we had been granted.

﹀☆✦✧

Taren and I talked dead honest about our future life together, about our hopes and our dreams. Richard and I were only scheduled to be on the island for two more days. Therefore, my love and I had many details to go over and iron out. At times, our conversation was almost like a negotiation of terms.

It turned out that Taren owned the resort and a good part of the island. We would live in the large house a little distance away from the hustle and bustle of the hotel. That fabulous mansion even had a view of the mountains of the Olympic Peninsula, a place I totally loved! Having a home like that had been one of my dreams!

We made a lot of decisions that day, including that we would have my lawyer draw up a prenup. Not that I thought that I would ever need one, but Taren wanted to make sure that I would be taken care of in any event. He gained more of my admiration and respect every day.

Here was a man who actually had my best interest at heart, who looked out for me! That felt incredibly good!

Once we had worked out a lot of the specifics, that large bed in our cabin began to assert its draw. Since making love to one's mate bound a shapeshifter irrevocably and forever to that person, doing the act before the actual wedding was frowned upon.

Since my change on the night of the full moon, the guidelines also applied to me. Taren and I were expected to behave ourselves. We would have to abstain from actually going all the way, not easy, given the intense attraction between us! It was hard to keep our hands off each other!

Not that our association was following any rules to start with! Fate seemed to have had a mind of its own when it threw us together. Our bond was already firmly in place! Could it still be broken? Doubtful!

My mate and I ended up cuddling on the bed and kissing until early evening. It took all our self-control not to go further, and just to be safe, we left all our clothes on. It felt so wonderful to be close to him, to be held in his loving embrace, to have him all to myself.

I could not imagine that we could feel even more connected, but Taren had assured me we would. Once our marriage had been officially conducted and consummated, we would be almost as one!

We would be able to read each other's minds, to always know what the other was feeling. We would have a bond so strong that we could easily find each other in a large crowd or in the deep woods in the midst of the night. Our love would flow freely between us. Now that alone sounded heavenly!

Looking at the gorgeous man before me, I was totally in awe of my good fortune. The love and life that were in my future were something I had thought existed only in my visions and tales.

I was still filled with absolute amazement that some of my wildest dreams were becoming reality!

I was genuinely looking forward to the journey to come, to our life together! There would be challenges, there always are, but we would deal with them together!

Chapter 19

Double Engagement

Taren and I decided that it was time to get going. We double-checked the anchor and secured the hatch. My mate took my hand and helped me down the steps and then into the dinghy. Not that I could not do this on my own, but I adored his courteousness.

Having someone look out for me like this made me feel loved and cherished. I had always acted so strong in the past that I had possibly denied any man in my life the opportunity to treat me with such gallantry, a mistake I would never repeat.

Once we were underway, I moved closer to Taren. He smiled at me and put his arm around my shoulders. The sense of happiness and contentment that filled me was beyond description.

I was sure that there would be an occasional spat in our future but as long as being together felt this connected, this right, this peaceful, and we were willing to work together to resolve any disagreements between us, we would be just fine.

Besides, we had to work things out. Splitting up with the bond we shared was not a viable option! It would definitely be an adventure, and I was looking forward to exploring life with this amazing man by my side.

⚜

I watched the island approach as Taren competently steered the boat towards shore. After the dinghy was secured to the floating dock jutting out from a small beach below the cliffs, we started on our way up to the hotel.

Once we reached the resort, my love and I headed for our individual suites. We needed to get ready for the evening meal. Within minutes, I had undone most of the damage from Taren's, and my time spent cuddling, but my face needed just a little bit more touchup. I wanted to look my absolute best.

My brother was nowhere in sight. I was surprised that he was not in our suite. Now, this was unusual, he usually waited for me, but since he was so in love with Marie, I figured that Richard wanted to spend every possible minute with her. I was sure that we would all meet up in the dining room.

Quickly, I changed into one of the beautiful, long dresses I had brought with me and ran a brush through my hair. Then, I added just a touch of sparkling lip gloss and refreshed my eyeshadow and mascara. All that kissing had not taken as heavy a toll on my makeup as I had first feared.

⚜

When I sat down at our table in the dining room, Taren had not yet arrived, but Richard and Marie were bouncing with excitement. They had taken a second look at the house my brother had come to see as his next home and had decided that they really liked it. The pair had great news. They had contacted the owner and had made an offer! They were now hoping that it would be accepted.

I was so happy for them and told them that I really hoped that they would get the place and that it would all work out beautifully. These two deserved to be happy. I was so preoccupied with their announcement that, at first, I did not notice the very palpable air of expectation in the room.

The staff seemed to have something special planned and told us in no uncertain terms that the clothes we were dressed in were nice for regular evenings but just would not do for tonight. They had put in a lot of extra effort, and they expected us to honor it by showing up in our finest garb.

We were happy to oblige them. Marie, Richard, and I went upstairs, laughing. We had decided that since the lady and I were of a very similar built, she could just wear one of my more formal dresses instead of returning to her own home to fetch one. And, besides, it would be more fun to get ready together!

Marie and I helped each other with some more elaborate makeup and put on jewelry. When we felt that we had primped enough to please the staff, we headed for the living area of the suite. Both Richard and Taren were already present.

The two men had their heads together and were talking in low voices. When they heard us close the bedroom door behind us, they jumped apart guiltily. I saw Richard unobtrusively slide something into his pocket. Marie and I looked at each other. What were they up to this time?

<hr>

I don't think any of us were prepared for what the capricious staff had in mind. We were greeted at the door to the dining hall and lined up, side by side. Each lady was handed a rose corsage and asked to place her hand on her partner's arm. When everything was arranged to Jeffrey and Allen's satisfaction, they threw open the double doors.

The entire room had been redecorated in just those few minutes. It now resembled an intimate restaurant and was lit only by candles. A low platform had been set up in the far corner, and a string quartet was playing soft music. Heavenly scented flowers had been placed in large vases along the walls. The whole space looked and smelled positively magical!

We had four waiters this night instead of just Jeffrey. They very formally pulled out our chairs for us. Once we were seated, each of us was presented with our favorite drink. Mine was a Pina Colada, and Taren's a Margarita. Since we liked both, we smiled at each other. Without needing to say a word, we had decided to share.

A few minutes later, the first course arrived, a creamy white asparagus soup. This was followed a short time after by filet mignon, new potatoes, and green beans tossed in a delicious garlic butter sauce. As if all that was not enough, we were served a plate of white asparagus and Black Forest ham to go along with the rest.

All the portions were just the right size to leave room for dessert. We each had a different one, and I loved my Crème Brule, especially since it was covered in a mountain of whipped cream!

By the time all the food was consumed, and the dishes were cleared away, none of us wanted to move. The four of us were only too happy to keep on talking. Also, it seemed that some sort of an encore was in the offing. I was good with anything just as long as it was not any more edibles!

I watched as Jeffrey brought in an ice bucket with what looked like Champaign. I was curious and a little amused. What did they have planned?

The entire evening's festivities had been entirely unexpected. Everything so far had been delightful and designed to make us feel very special. The staff had truly gone out of their way to create not only a magical atmosphere but also a superb meal. Neither Marie nor I had a clue that the best was yet to come.

A while ago, the band had switched to playing some of my favorite love songs. They had just started playing 'A Time for Love,' and I could not help but tap along with the melody. I was so enthralled by the music that I completely missed the wordless exchange between my brother and Taren. Marie's sharp elbow brought me back to the present, and, just in time!

Richard and Taren, looking so handsome in their black tuxedos, rose from their chairs and bowed to us. Then my brother got down on one knee in front of his lady. I could feel my throat closing up with emotions.

Taren nodded to my brother. Richard looked lovingly up at Marie. Then, he solemnly took her hand. Gazing into her eyes, he held out a small box containing a diamond ring he had just pulled out of his pocket.

How had he managed to lay his hands on a ring? Here on the island? Taren must have had something to do with that! The conversation Marie and I had interrupted in our suite took on a whole new meaning. They had planned this together!

Richard cleared his throat. I could tell that he was choked up with excitement and the love he was feeling. He spoke the solemn words so many ladies have longed to hear all over the world throughout the ages. "Marie Celeste O'Chaudecy, will you do me the great honor of becoming my wife, to allow me to walk beside you from this day on?"

Tears were in both of their eyes as she whispered, "Nothing would please me more." Richard slid the ring on Marie's delicate hand, and she reached out to him and buried her face in his shoulder. It took her a few minutes to regain her composure.

Finding love again had been as unexpected for her as it had been for my brother, and she was so happy that she was overcome with emotions.

Richard now turned to Taren and waved for him to proceed. My love stepped forward and got down on one knee just as my brother had done a few minutes ago. He gently reached out for my left hand and placed a sensual kiss in my palm. My pulse and breathing instantly increased at his touch.

"Ella Janine Montgomery, would you do me the honor of becoming my wife, to allow me to love and care for you from this day onward, to walk beside you?" At his words, tears of pure joy started rolling down my cheeks.

My throat was so tight that all I could do was nod as I looked down on this man who was to me the most gorgeous I had ever seen. He was everything I had ever wanted, had dreamed of, and as he slid a magnificent diamond ring on my finger, I could not suppress a happy sob.

Not caring any longer what anyone thought, Taren pulled me towards him. Before I knew it, I ended up sitting on his knee with my arms around his neck, kissing the man I would spend the rest of my life with like I could not get enough of him ever.

A loud pop followed by clapping and cheering brought us back to our senses. None of us had noticed that the entire staff of the resort, plus some of the island's other residents, had quietly sneaked in just as soon as they were given the signal that the proposals were about to take place!

Champaign glasses were pushed into our hands, and when everyone present had something to drink, our favorite waiter, Jeffrey, raised his glass in a toast.

"Long and joyful wedded bliss full of love and happiness to Taren and Ella StClair and Richard and Marie Montgomery! May their lives be happy, and may they never be blue!"

"Hear! Hear!" echoed through the room before everyone took a drink in our honor.

❧❧❧

The rest of the evening turned into an exuberant celebration. Word of our engagements spread across the island like wildfire. Within minutes, more musicians arrived, and tables and chairs were pushed to the side to clear a space for dancing. I believe that almost the entire community ended up rejoicing with us!

Taren and I and Richard and Marie shared the first dance. The band played 'Walk Beside Me' which earned them a grateful smile from me. I love that song! In just a few words, it sums up what a relationship should be.

The rest of the revelers watched and clapped to the beat. It turned out to be a truly magical night, just like something out of one of the movies of old!

Later, as I was dancing a slow song with Taren, held tightly in his loving arms, I could not help but marvel how gracious fate had been. It had brought me here, to this magical moment. I was so happy that I felt like I was floating on cloud nine.

Here I was, after all the heartache I had been through, after almost giving up hope to ever have that special someone to share my days with, truly blessed to be celebrating the promise of a life together with this magnificent man!

Chapter 20

The Mainland

The next two days went by in a blur. I had never been so happy in my entire life. I was engaged to be married to the love of my life! Among other things, he was affectionate, kind, respectful, smart, and he adored me. He loved to sail, and his eyes sparkled with happiness and laughter. And, he truly saw ME, the person I am, and loved and admired me for it. How much more could one woman ask for?

Each morning, Richard, Marie, Taren, and I would meet up for breakfast. Then, each couple would head out for adventures on their own. We would meet up for lunch and then do something together. Taren was a fabulous tour guide and showed us some of the hidden nook and crannies of the beautiful island.

My brother and I learned much about the history of the place and its inhabitants. It was important to Taren and Marie that we were fully informed and that no secrets remained. They took great pains to tell us all the details of the past and present of the shapeshifters' society. It was important to both that we would feel at home upon our return.

˙·٭҉٭·˙

Richard and Marie had also worked out their future together. As I had hoped, my brother would be moving to this beautiful island as well. Matter of fact, his offer had been accepted, and he had already put down a down payment on the house he liked so much! His lady had agreed to make it their home.

Taren had suggested that the couple could stay with us in our home, it was big enough after all. My brother and his fiancé had refused. They did not want to intrude and felt that as newlyweds, they would be more comfortable in a place of their own.

˙·٭҉٭·˙

My heart was sad when I packed the rest of my things on the day we would be returning to our prospective residences. Richard was going back to Seattle and me, to Gig Harbor. Those houses, as much as we loved them, were no longer our homes since our hearts would be left behind here on this island.

George, our very round chef, had gone out of his way to spoil us on our last morning. He had served up so much food that the four of us were unable to eat it all. Undeterred, the jovial man packed the rest in a cooler and sent it with us.

After many tearful goodbyes, we were finally off. We took the carriage down to the ferry and were soon steaming back towards Anacortes.

˙·٭҉٭·˙

Taren and Marie had decided to come with us. None of us could bear to be parted from our new partners. Lunch on the top deck turned into a long and lively affair. We were having a wonderful time, and our laughter resounded across the sunlit water.

The boat had been decorated by the staff and now resembled more a wedding barge than a serious ferry. This garnered us lots of attention as we were chugging along. People cheered and waved, and we were only too happy to return their greetings and well wishes.

When we reached Anacortes later that day, we said goodbye to the crew, and the four of us piled into the limo. Good thing that it had a double seat or one of us would have had to ride up front instead of being able to sit next to their partner! As it was, we were all in high spirits, and the drive to Richard's house passed rather quickly.

Traffic on I5 on the way to Gig Harbor would still be fairly bad at this hour, so the four of us headed out to dinner instead. We had a leisurely meal in a nearby Thai restaurant before returning to Richard's home and saying goodbye.

Carlo, the chauffeur, had declined to join us, and by the time we returned, Taren's and my luggage had already been loaded into my RAV. We were ready to head for home. Having total trust in my fiancé, I handed him the keys to my car.

·⚜·⚜·

The drive was uneventful and, since we were busy making more plans for the future, it went much faster than usual. Still, it was pretty late by the time we arrived. As per our agreement, the friend who had taken over watching the pets from John these last couple of days, had locked up and had gone home once I had told her that we were on the way.

We would see Cecilia the next day so that I could introduce my fiancé to her. I could not wait and knew that she would just love him! How could she not? He was everything and more she had hoped I would find!

The dogs were absolutely ecstatic to see us. They had missed me as much or maybe more than I had them. I had to let them out and greet them several times before we could make it through the door. Even then, they kept running around us like mad things.

To my amazement, my usually standoffish German Shepherd greeted Taren like a long-lost friend. She was whining, licking his hands, and rolled over in an invitation for him to rub her tummy. The little guy was no better, and my love ended up having to pick him up to appease the insistent little creature.

Taren even did well with the guinea pigs, and I was impressed with his affection towards them. It was official. My love was now part of the pack!

That night, we spent in separate bedrooms. Both of us were tired and feared for our self-control. The next morning, we went through and took an assessment of the garden and home. Taren made a list of things that needed to be done before the house could be rented.

As part of our agreement, we would be living in his home. He had made a will that stated that the large house, as well as the resort and the grounds, would become mine if anything ever happened to him. Taren was determined that I would be taken care of in all eventualities. He is a circumspect man who has only my best interest at heart, a true knight and hero!

We had decided not to sell the house. Taren, being the introspective and understanding man he was, wanted me to have options and to never feel trapped. I would have a place to return to if I so desired. Not that I thought that this was even a possibility, but I appreciated the sentiment none the less. It was nice to have choices.

Later that day, we went for a long hike in the nearby park. I wanted to share all the places I loved so much with my mate. There was much about living out here I would miss! The Key Peninsula is a beautiful area with some of my favorite haunts.

Another reason I had never moved before were my many friends. Jacqueline and I had been through much together; Cedric had always bailed me out when something went wrong with my home; Rae's house was my halfway stop on my walks; Cecilia was one of the most beautiful, honest and intuitive people I knew who often confirmed my own impressions; Rhonda, an amazing pianist, was not just my willing editor but also my rock; and Mary, sweet and gentle, was a real pleasure to be around.

Robbi and her family were just amazing and always made me feel like I was part of their clan. I loved each and every one of them, enjoyed the holidays with them, and was thrilled to be considered an aunt to the little ones.

Every one of these wonderful, remarkable people had always been there for me and cheered me on in all my endeavors. And, these were only some of the people I had come to love deeply while living out here! I would miss them!

My friends had been a treasured gift, as well as my lifeline. Whenever I had ended up heartbroken from an encounter with Andrew, they had comforted me. They had listened to my exuberant talks about my books and had shared my delight in my rapid spiritual growth, in my processing and letting go of the past.

I valued their opinion and their unwavering support. Each and every one of them was a true friend. No matter where life led me, all they ever wanted for me was the best. I deeply love each and every one of them and always will.

Taren promised me that we would come visit anytime I pleased and that there would always be room for them in our home or the resort. Knowing this made me feel a little better about moving.

⚘

I had called them all from the island using the landline and had given them the good news that I had met a caring, honest, sincere man. My friends had been delighted and could not wait to meet Taren. Their trust in me, in that I knew what I was doing, even so, this had happened so quickly, was heartwarming.

They had raised questions, and I had expected no less from these wonderful people. They would always look out for me. When I assured them that this was truly what I wanted and that I was genuinely loved by this new man in my life, they had rejoiced with me. It meant much to me that they were happy for me.

⚘

The next few days would be spent introducing Taren to my friends and family. I was sure that they would approve and come to love him. How could they not? He was amazing! And, they would like any man who treated me with the love, respect, and affection my wonderful fiancé did.

That we were actually already engaged was one fact I had withheld for the moment. It would have been too much to spring on them over the phone. Taren and I had decided to divulge this little detail once we saw them in person.

Let them meet my love first before sharing such excellent news with my unsuspecting family and friends!

⚘

As I had figured, Taren was an instant success, and every time we revealed our engagement, an impromptu celebration took place. My fiancé invited each one of them to our upcoming wedding and offered them a free room at the resort. He truly was just beyond incredible!

Then came the day we were to meet my son Steve and his lovely wife, Parichat. We had agreed to head to their business and to go to dinner together from there once they were able to get away. I was also looking forward to showing Taren what these two had built. I was so very proud of their achievements!

My son was a bit skeptical at first and spent some time giving Taren the first degree. I thought I was going to die of embarrassment when Steve eyed my love a few minutes after the introductions and asked him flat out. "What are your intentions towards my mother?"

Taren took it all in stride. He slid his arm around my waist and pulled me close. "I intend to marry her and make her the happiest woman alive." How was that for an answer? It sure pleased Steve! After that, my son and Taren got along famously, and Parichat liked him as well.

Meeting my daughter in person would have to wait. Since Alison really wanted to get to know Taren, we therefore decided to skype with her instead. A trip to Tennessee was just not something I foresaw in our immediate future, there was too much to do. I decided to rather fly her and her family out for the wedding. I was sure that she and especially my grandson would just love spending some time on the island.

⟿❧⟾

It took us a week to get through all the social obligations. Taren hired a carpenter to take care of some of the maintenance needed on the house. I had done my best on my own but had often felt a bit overwhelmed by all the little things that needed doing. Especially since that took time away from my writing!

I was extremely grateful to hand all those jobs over to someone else. My fiancé also hired a crew to deal with the yard. I was thrilled to watch them trim and prune the place back to some of its former glory. They were also kind enough to dig up some of my beloved roses, which would move to the island with us.

Writing was my bliss, not gardening. I had done a fair bit, but the place was too big for one person to take care of. And, it had already been somewhat overgrown when I had taken it over.

Therefore, I had resigned myself long ago that it would always be a fairy garden. Beautiful but just a bit wild. It made me happy to see it tamed a little.

⟿❧⟾

Then, the big day arrived. To say I was excited was putting it mildly. I was filled with a mixture of anxiety and anticipation because this was, after all, a huge step I was taking. The time had arrived to empty my house and get everything packed up for the move. I was pretty relieved when the truck showed up. I just wanted to get this part over with!

To my surprise, some of the staff members from the resort hopped out of the van. I was happy to see them, and warm greetings were exchanged all the way around. It took us most of the day to get everything boxed up and loaded. For a change, all I had to do was supervise. Even the cleaning was done for me! Now, this was a life I could get used to!

✦✦✦

By that evening, nothing remained in the house, and it was spotless. Taren and I wandered through the rooms hand in hand. I had been happy here; this home had been my healing place, but somehow, I had always known that one day, I would leave it behind.

I don't think I ever truly settled in completely. All the other places I had owned I had painted and made over to totally suit me but not this one. I loved and cherished it but had always seen it as borrowed somehow.

As I walked out the door and closed it behind me, I felt a pang of sadness. I would miss this house, and kind of wished that I could take it with me. But, this part of my life was over. A whole new era was about to begin.

✦✦✦

A chance for a happy life with my ex had been there, but it had not been part of the amazing future the Universe had planned for me. Looking back, I was actually glad that the opportunity had passed me by.

Life with Andrew had been an intense time of growth, one I would be forever grateful for, but it takes two to tango and to make a relationship thrive. We had attacked each other instead of the problems, something I would never allow again.

I was truly blessed to have found a man who would walk beside me, who saw me as his equal, while still understanding that at times, I would need him to be my shelter. We would be there for each other, and Taren was willing and able to fully return my love. Since I had seen the other side of that coin, I had no problem recognizing this as the treasure and gift that it was.

I had dreamed of love all my life, I had written about it, felt it, sensed it, but until I had met Taren, it had only seen hints of what could be. I was immensely grateful to have the privilege to experience a true love such as this.

After one last stroll through the garden, Taren and I loaded the pets into my car. As we drove away into that amazing new life that was dawning on the horizon, I took one final look back. I placed a spell of protection on the house and grounds in thanks for the shelter it had granted me. It was the least I could do.

My fiancé would handle the renting out part for me. He was determined to find just the right fit. I actually suspected that he already had someone in mind.

Chapter 21

The Return Home

Taren and I returned to the island, this time with pets and possessions in tow. My dogs immediately took off to explore the house and grounds once we let them out of the car. My fiancé assured me that they would be safe. I had observed his astounding ability to communicate with these two, and my mind was instantly at ease.

Under his gentle guidance, Arianna, my skittish German Shepherd, had come a long way in just a few days. I was so thrilled! She actually got along with other dogs now! As it was, my furry mates did not go very far and ended up racing exuberantly around the car like two crazy things.

To my immense surprise and pleasure, an enclosure for the guinea pigs had already been prepared in the home. My considerate mate also had a safe outside playpen built for the boys! I was so grateful to Taren for thinking of that! I really was blessed to have him in my life!

After being cooped up in their cage for most of the day, my little guys were only too happy to check out their new run. It seemed to meet with their full approval, and soon, they were exuberantly bouncing around. I would move them inside later once we had gotten settled.

To me, it felt like coming home. Just the feeling as I set foot back on the island had been incredible. Now that I had been gone a few days, I could clearly feel the magic singing in my blood.

✦

The home I would be moving into in a few weeks was big and already furnished, but the guest cottage had been mostly emptied. We had decided that this was where I would be staying until the wedding which was planned for the beginning of September.

The house was charming and had three-bedrooms, very much like the one I had left behind. The view was gorgeous and would be an inspiration for my writing, as was my ever-growing love for Taren. I knew that I would be comfortable and happy there, especially with my mate close by.

The resort staff carried in all my possessions and placed them wherever I wanted. With their help, it did not take me and my little pack long to get settled in.

✦

I soon fell into a pleasant routine. Get up, go for a walk with Taren and the dogs, have breakfast at the resort, go home and write. My love usually came and got me for lunch because he had noticed that time slipped right past me once I got to working. It is easy for me to forget to eat.

Taren would accompany me back home after the meal, sneak in a few kisses and leave me to my own devices once again until it was time for the dogs' afternoon hike. To give me time to finish the book, he was actually handling most of the plans for the wedding!

We would have dinner and spend some more time together, sometimes watching a movie or just talking. I was going to bed now at a more reasonable hour and no longer working until all hours in the morning.

Being in such a peaceful setting without having to worry about gardening and maintenance and such, I finished and published the book I had been working on in record time. To say I was thrilled is putting it mildly.

My wonderful fiancé took over from there. Having managed the resort and several other estates, he had great connections. These he now used to market not just this one but all of my books!

⚘

Beyond following my bliss of spinning tales, I was getting ready for the wedding and the subsequent move into the much larger house. I was looking forward to living with Taren, but I really liked my 'little cottage' as he called it. I had made myself very comfortable and would especially miss the nook I had set up for writing.

I had placed my couch right in front of a west-facing window. Every time I glanced up, I could see the magnificent mountains, especially now in the summer with this fabulous weather. Sometimes, when it was foggy, only the tops would peak out, but even then, it was a glorious view!

Realizing that I really liked my workspace, my thoughtful love promised to take the entire setup and find the perfect spot for it in my new home! This earned him a big hug and a passionate kiss with the promise of more to come once we were married.

⚘

Taren was the most attentive and considerate fiancé any woman could ever ask for. If I wanted something, all I had to do was make a mention. He was observant and really listened. His empathy and compassion allowed him an understanding of my needs that stunned me. He often knew what I required before I did!

Since life and relationships are all about give and take, I watched Taren carefully to make sure that I returned his mindfulness in equal measure. I really enjoyed surprising him with little acts of thoughtfulness and kindness. It soon became apparent that he was as unused to this as I was.

⁘

October through April could be very dreary and cold in the islands. It was nice to have a warm spot available. Therefore, we were searching for a place to escape to for a few months in the winter when the weather was at its worst. I had been confined to a wheelchair years ago, and Taren felt that sunshine and warmth when it was frigid here would be a good thing for me.

For days, the wonderful man presented me with house after house to choose from. Some in the Hawaiian Islands, some in southern California, Florida, and even in the Caribbean. All were beautiful but some more so than others. One of my concerns was to find a place where the pets would be safe.

We would go over these homes every evening, pondering each residence's pros and cons. Finally, we found a place on Kauai we both liked. It had a fantastic view of the ocean and was close to a path for our daily exercise. In other words, perfect!

⁘

Taren contacted the realtor and, the next thing I knew, it was time to look at the house in person. My love booked our flights and hotel, and we set out for the island. To say that I was excited was putting it mildly!

I was not only thrilled to be able to check out our prospective winter residence but also happy to return to Kauai. I had fallen in love with the place during the time I had spent there with Andrew, and I was looking forward to seeing my friends!

This was to be a short trip; we would stay for only three days. Definitely too much traveling and too exhausting for the pets. They were happy here in their new home and comfortable enough by now for us to go without them.

Jeffrey, who loved the dogs, had volunteered to look after our little pack. I was relieved to be able to leave them in his competent hands.

⋆⋆⋆⋆⋆⋆

The other decision we had to make was where to go for our honeymoon. Taren, wanting to spoil me, brought up so many choices! He was willing to show me any place in the world I desired to see.

He would have been happy to take me to Rome, Venice, London, or Paris, or some of the other locations we had explored in my dreams. But, my instincts told me that it would be better if we stayed closer to home this time and saved those trips for later. I also knew that he really wanted to try out his new boat! And, to be honest, so did I!

That gorgeous vessel was sitting right down the cliffs waiting for us. The *Mermaid* was really calling to me! We had taken her out for a couple of day trips but no extended sails as of yet. I felt that it was about time to put her through her paces.

I finally managed to convince Taren that this was what I really wanted to do on our honeymoon. Actually, there was nothing I was going to love more than going sailing with my mate in the San Juans. September could be rainy, but we would still have a great time since we would be together.

⋆⋆⋆⋆⋆⋆

He was the one who suggested that we should take the pets. I had been prepared to leave them home just this once but was not fond of that idea. We were walking through the foyer of the hotel at the time when he mentioned this. At those words, I came to a dead stop. Tears had formed in my eyes, and I was overwhelmed with emotions.

Not caring who was around, I rushed over to him and threw myself into his arms. It was not until that moment that he realized the true magnitude of the gift he had just given me. I was so happy that I ended up crying and smiling all at the same time!

I love the San Juans, and there were many places I had longed to visit again. I was looking forward to making new memories, to long hikes on almost deserted islands, to searching for sea glass on Cypress, to evenings cuddled up close together on deck watching the sun go down, surrounded by my little pack which now included Taren. To me, that was heaven, pure bliss!

In August, my brother and Marie came over from the mainland to attend the full moon ceremony. After the end of the bonfire celebration, we quietly slipped away to the circle. There were tourists about, and we did not want to attract their attention.

It was Richard's turn to take the elixir. He had no expectations and knew going in that even if he never learned how to shift, the brew would still grant him healing and long life. However, to his absolute delight, he turned into a large fox.

To her surprise, Marie actually had an easier time shifting than ever before. The four of us set out to spend the night running and playing in the woods.

Somehow, Taren and I ended up alone in the cove with the kayaks and sailboats. Both of us changed back into humans at the same moment. We knew just what the other was feeling and thinking, we needed no words to communicate.

Hand in hand and stark naked, we walked into the sea. My fiancé had other shapes besides the handsome wolf he could turn into, as did most of the other shifters. So far, however, I had only transformed into an owl. I was determined to find out what else I could do. I already had something in mind.

Taren hesitated just a moment before turning into a large dolphin. I stood there a little longer, shivering as the cold water undulated against my bare body. I had always wanted to be a mermaid. Would it be possible? How wonderful it would feel to glide through the water without the need of any kind of breathing apparatus, driven along by a powerful tail!

Was my imagination the limit, or were there other boundaries that would constrain my shapeshifting? I had never thought to ask until now! I decided that it was worth a try, all that could happen was that I would not succeed.

It turned out that where there is a will, there is a way. At least this seemed to apply to shapeshifting on this magical island. That night, I flew through the waves driven onward by my beautiful tail, I danced through the kelp, I raised my voice in song to the moon. My faithful dolphin raced along beside me. We met up with my friend, the orca, and dove deep in his wake.

Having tired of one form, I decided to explore another. Turning into a killer whale did not seem like a wise choice since this would have startled the orca. I turned over several ideas in my mind but discarded one after the other until I finally homed in on an acceptable shape.

Next thing I knew, I was a playful sea otter.

The trouble began when Taren shifted his own shape to match mine. Soon, we were racing each other around the bay in the light of the full moon. I was smaller and more agile and had quickly figured out how to turn on a dime. To his delight, I managed to give my love a merry chase.

When he finally caught me, our play turned into something else altogether. Desire set my blood on fire when he accidentally rubbed up against me.

The brief contact seemed to have a similar effect on Taren! We moved closer together, weaving around each other in our sleek otter shapes, touching more with each passing minute.

Before long, our intertwining of bodies became more and more urgent. The iron control we had as humans went out the window in animal shape. That night, in sea otter form, we truly became one for the very first time.

By mutual consent, we headed back towards shore. As if a dam had been broken, we switched to human shape and made love in the moonlit surf. The extasy that man took me to that night was beyond description. I exploded into the light, floated helplessly among the stars. I felt no cold, no pain, and the sand that was intruding into all kinds of places only presented a minor irritant that was not even worthy of notice.

I could have stayed right there forever, but we decided that there were more comfortable places to explore each other's bodies. We ended up racing home to my cottage, enjoyed a hot shower together, and took up right where we had left off down at the beach.

We could not get enough of each other, did not want to stop touching, discovering, making love. Good thing that Taren had more stamina than most!

Since our unbreakable bond had already been formed, we considered for a moment to just come clean and move my things over early. But in the end, we decided to respect decorum and keep up the pretense.

If we thought for a moment that we were fooling anyone, we were delusional. Our friends knew us only too well and quickly caught onto our little game. To their credit, they turned a blind eye and did not say a word. They left us our belief that no one was aware of our secret late-night rendezvous.

We should have known better! After all, how can one possibly hide one's sneaking about on an island full of wily shapeshifters?

Chapter 22

The Wedding

Finally, the day of the wedding dawned. Taren and I were both relieved as well as excited. We had behaved ourselves these last couple of days, but it had not been easy. Most of our guests had already arrived, and entirely too many people were present at the resort, the cottage, and the house to manage our sneaking about and clandestine trysts.

I was so happy that I could not stop smiling. All of my closest friends and my entire family were here to celebrate our upcoming marriage with Taren and I. Carlo had been picking up people from all over the place for days and had been to the airport several times.

That morning, Marie and my girlfriends helped me get dressed. We had a whole lot of fun and shared much laughter. The ladies did my hair and makeup. Jacquie is really an expert, and between her and my brother's fiancé, they made me look like a beautiful fairytale princess.

The long, stylish, pure white wedding gown was stunning. Elegant but with a sense of the whimsical. The bodice was tight past the waist where it flared out and just flowed like silken water down to the floor. Several petticoats helped to cleverly maintain the smooth, classic lines of the dress and allowed it to fall just right. The moment I had laid eyes on this gorgeous creation, I had known that it was perfect for me.

The ceremony was to start at 11 AM. I was so excited that I could barely sit still while my friends addressed those last-minute touches they felt just needed to be added here and there. They would try something, discuss it, and most often change their minds. The stylish simplicity of my ensemble was hard to improve on.

I think they were almost as happy as I was about my good fortune. Every one of them heartily approved of my future husband. We were all looking forward to the upcoming ceremony, especially since it promised to be very different from anything we had ever attended.

I could not wait to officially start my new life with Taren! Every few minutes, my eyes would stray to the clock. Never before had time moved so very slowly! I was starting to think we would never get there at all!

I was therefore greatly relieved when Richard, looking very distinguished and handsome in his tailored suit, came to get me. My brother guided me towards the entrance of the hotel, where Jeffrey was keeping an eye out for us. My girlfriends, who followed behind us, now dashed through the doors and into the waiting carriage.

Once the others were off, a beautifully decorated coach pulled up in the driveway. I was absolutely delighted but also deeply touched! What effort had been made to create such a perfect vision! The entire hansom was decorated with white roses, and even the horses were white and were wearing wreaths made of the same flawless roses.

Jeffrey was immensely pleased when he saw my reaction, and I thanked him expansively as he escorted us out to the vehicle. He was positively beaming as he helped me into my seat. Once he had jumped onto the back to act as a footman, he gave the signal for us to get on our way.

The weather was glorious, warm with a pleasant breeze coming off the cool water. We had considered having the ceremony outside, but Angelique had insisted that it was to be held in the old church where every shapeshifter before us had spoken their bond. We had finally relented and let her have her way.

A few minutes later, we pulled up in front of the ancient chapel. It was just large enough to hold all our family and friends. Jeffrey helped me out of the carriage and, like an old mother hen, made sure that everything about me was in its place and perfect. Only then did he open one of the doors and poked his head in to let the assembly know that we had arrived.

Finally, the first clear notes of the wedding march could be heard. Jeffrey gave us a nod, and we got ready. He and our coachman threw open the doors.

Richard proudly walked me down the aisle of the small church. The rehearsal had been held at the resort. I had therefore never laid eyes on this magnificent old building, which made this incredible setting all the more of a surprise as well as more special.

It was obvious that the chapel was ancient, and it was absolutely glorious. The ends and tops of the pews were elaborately carved with all sorts of animals and plants. All the wood in the building had been polished until it shone. I loved the rich hue of the seats and the way it contrasted with the pale rock of the floor.

To me, it looked like the tiles were a light-colored sandstone. The effect was both stunning as well as earthy and, in a way, very pagan.

The most superb pieces in the entire building, however, where the windows, especially the one right behind the white granite altar. When I first caught sight of it, I almost came to a dead stop.

In the very back of the church, above the altar, was a huge stained-glass window. The background was clear and at its very center was a picture contained in a large circle. A handsome man looked down upon us from his perch far above. His image was, separated by about a foot and a half of smaller, clear, glass panes, surrounded by slighter circles that contained different animals. Elaborate green vines spanned the distance between the pictures and wove their way decoratively over parts of this striking creation.

The effect was stunning, especially for those of us who knew about the shapeshifters. And, right below this spectacular piece of art stood Taren, outlined with light from above.

~ ❦ ~

Once I laid eyes on my future husband, everything else faded away. Richard proudly walked me down the aisle, and he was smiling from ear to ear as he presented my hand to Taren. He and my fiancé were becoming very good friends which delighted me to no end.

I looked up at this man I was going to spend the rest of my days with and once again thought how gorgeous he was. I was so blessed to have him in my life. Our eyes locked, and the world fell away.

The draw, this incredible magnetism between us kicked into high gear. A church filled with people was not the best time for such a reaction! I could see that Taren had a hard time restraining himself from pulling me close right then and there.

A persistent throat clearing finally got our attention. Our friend, the island's priestess, was getting impatient. Angelique was ready to get started. She was going to marry us following the ancient shifter tradition. Being so mesmerized by Taren, I do not remember much of the ceremony only that there was a mysterious power in the seeress' words.

I could feel the intense bond we already shared tighten further. When a shapeshifter agreed to mate for life, they meant it. There would be no divorce, no abandoning the relationship. The only viable option was to work through disagreements. I really liked that.

I suspected, however, that our bonds would last long beyond our mortal lives. My gut told me that Taren and my fate had been tied together from this day onward through all eternity and that we would stand in front of a similar altar again multiple times in the future.

I was happy knowing that Taren would be my partner again in the next life and the ones after that. Having my love returned so fully, so completely was addicting at best!

The celebration which followed our vows was a real affirmation of life and the most fun wedding party I had ever attended. After the ceremony, all of us returned to the resort. The staff had hurried ahead, and everything was in readiness by the time the guests arrived back at the hotel.

The food, as always, was superb. The first course was a hearty soup, followed by the most tender prime rib I have ever tasted. With it we were served rice, potatoes, pasta, and a number of different vegetables to choose from. It was truly a feast!

Desert was as also heavenly, and then the wedding cake was rolled into the room. Now here was a real work of art! A picture of Taren and I decorated the very top of the three tiers. It was surrounded by vines that reminded me vividly of the stained-glass in the church!

Golden wedding bells ornamented the tops of the lower two tiers, and here as well, green vines wove their way around the outside. This sweet creation was so beautiful that I almost felt bad when Taren's and mine joined hands made that first cut.

It turned out to taste just as heavenly as it looked, and it was gluten-free!

✦✦✦

Our wedding party made a lasting impression on everyone present and lasted long into the night. Several of the island's talented musicians had insisted on playing, and the Celtic music that filled the air stirred the blood in all those present. Most ended up dancing for who could resist such a captivating melody and rousing rhythm?

The excellent wine we made on the island flowed freely, and by late evening, the party was in full swing. Nobody noticed as Taren and I quietly slipped away and made our way home. We had other things on our minds besides dancing!

✦✦✦

Our guests loved their time on the island. The magic of the land did its job and they all left with a sense of distinct wellbeing. The ones we knew needed extra healing; we would invite back. My friend Cecilia actually agreed to take up residence in the cottage. She would look after the pets whenever we could not take them on our travels.

Her health had improved so drastically while visiting with us that she was reluctant to leave. She decided that she would go see her family and other friends at times but was happy to make her home with us on the island.

An additional incentive for her to stay was her budding romance with one of our residents. The talented and kindhearted man had taken quite an interest in her, and I had noticed that the feeling was mutual.

✦✦✦

After the wedding, we went on our honeymoon. Taren and I had a wonderful time. We anchored a lot and spent many hours making love. We made new, happy memories of the islands I adored so much. The dogs were delighted with the long hikes we went on. After making sure that we had Cypress all to ourselves, both Taren and I shifted to wolves, and the four of us ran as a pack. Eagle Cliff Outlook was much easier to climb on four feet!

We spent almost a month just going from one place to another and frequently returned to Doe Bay and its hot tubs. What a delight to soak in that steaming, mineral-rich mountain water, especially once the weather turned cold!

When everything settled down, I finished the sequel to my Highlands series. I intended to take a little time off, but all of a sudden, I felt prompted to write down and share the incredible story of Taren and me. No one would believe that the events were actually true unless they had been there and all those who had been kept mum.

As I started this book, I remembered the scenes I had been shown on that rock that first day my love and I had officially met. Those visions had assured me that Taren would always do his best to treat me right and not hurt me. Even then, I had already trusted him completely.

Just the thought brought tears to my eyes. What a difference to my previous partners! How wonderful to have no need to protect myself from the person I loved most! To be able to feel totally safe! I never stopped being grateful for that.

I am hoping that this modern-day fairytale will touch your heart and bring you hope that true love is out there waiting for you.

All you have to do is believe.

Appendix

The People

Alexander: The manager of the hotel, at times a rather arrogant and haughty man, but he has a good heart and is extremely loyal to Taren.

Allen: The maître d'hôtel of Wolf Haven Resort, an attractive, tall, slender man.

Andrew: Ella's ex-boyfriend, whom she loved very deeply. For a long time, she was heartbroken over their breakup.

Arianna: Ella's rescued German Shepherd.

Angelique: She is a gypsy, seeress, and the high priestess of the island.

Carlo: The chauffeur who picks up Ella and her brother from Richard's home.

Cecilia: Ella's friend and one of the most beautiful, honest, and intuitive people she knew.

Cedric: Ella's friend who bailed her out any time something went wrong with her house. They also liked to go on adventures together.

Ella Janine Montgomery: The heroine of the story, an accomplished writer, editor, publisher, and much more.

George: The rotund cook of the resort, a jovial and kind man.

Jacqueline: She and Ella went through much together. Ella genuinely appreciated her unwavering support of her meandering journey.

Jeffrey: A waiter at the resort.

John: Ella's house sitter and friend in Gig Harbor. The pets adore him, and he has a tendency to spoil them rotten. John is an accomplished author, as well as a knight. He was giving Ella sword fighting lessons.

Marie Celeste O'Chaudecy: A brilliant pianist, violinist, and flutist. She works at the resort as a maid to pass the time. The lady was beautiful with her delicate features and long black hair. She was talented and smart and fell deeply in love with Richard.

Micha: Ella's dachshund/chihuahua mix. He is a trained service dog and has traveled all over with Ella.

Rae: One of Ella's friends who she loves talking to and who she frequently visited when she was out walking the dogs.

Richard Montgomery: The brother and one of the best friends of Ella's.

Rhonda: One of Ella's close friends, she helps with the editing of her books.

Robbi: One of Ella's friends, she also helps with the editing and has adopted Ella into her family.

Taren StClair: The shapeshifter and Ella's dream lover. The name Taren is of Gaelic origin and means 'Thunder.'

Thomas: The maître d' of the resort.

Places

Fair Haven Village: a collection of 13 whimsical homes. Ella's brother, Richard, and his fiancé Marie end up buying a home here.

Wolf Haven Resort: The resort Ella and Richard are invited to visit. The theme of the place is 'Scotland of Old,' and the music and costumes of the staff reflect this. The setting of the place is magnificent, and its terrace has a view of the beautiful Olympic Mountains.

The Island: The island is a magical place where the shapeshifters have made their home for generations now. Its incredible healing ability does not only extend to people but also to itself.

Afterword

I love to write, and even the tiniest little bit of an impression or glimpse can give rise to a story or poem. Sometimes a new tale will pop in my head while walking, reading a book, watching a movie, or in a dream. Since I have learned how to look, stories are all around me, begging to be shared with the world.

I especially cherish the ideas coming to me in my dreams. The ones I remember vividly feel different. When I put them down on paper, more details flow into my mind, almost as if I had lived them. If there are many universes and many dimensions, who knows, maybe in one of those I did.

Many of my tales started with a dream, as did this one. On September 1st of 2019, while I was helping Patton Boyle prepare his book 'The Peaceable Kingdom' for publication, I had this incredible dream. It was of a woman meeting this gorgeous man who could shift into a wolf. That was what started this story.

Then, I went on a date and met Richard. Now, I had the perfect older brother! On the 9th of September 2019, I sat down and started writing/channeling the tale. It came out fast and furious, and I finished the first draft in less than six days! To me this was incredible!

The initial and main edit went really fast as well since it had been written fairly cleanly and needed few edits. Somehow, the Universe gave me until Sunday the following week to get the book done. Proof copies were to be printed that day! But if that meant staying in the flow, I was going to do it! I actually managed to upload the book one day ahead!

This is the very first book that I have ever written in the first person. It was incredibly fun to weave fantasy and reality together into something truly magical, especially since it is set in the San Juan Islands, a place I dearly love!

The story captured my imagination, and I was on fire. Never before have I finished a project as quickly as this one nor one that spoke to me on such an intimate level.

For me, writing is just as exciting as reading. I know where I am going, but, along the way, most of my stories manage to surprise me. As I am writing along, new adventures which I never even expected flow from my fingertips, and I can't wait to see where it is taking me. This keeps me enthralled and working away. Writing for me is almost like automatic writing or channeling, and I am always eager to find out just what happens next. I had a fabulous time writing this book and hope you will enjoy reading it as much as I loved writing it.

This will be my third book to see publication. I believe in Divine timing and that there is a reason for everything. I intend to turn this story into an audiobook at some time in the future for your listening pleasure.

Much love

GC Sinclaire

Acknowledgements

A huge thank you to the Universe for sending me Taren in my dream just when I needed him most. In this modern-day fairytale, I learned what love can feel like - exhilarating, magnetizing, energizing, but also comforting and safe.

I am grateful to my 'brother' Richard Weeks and wonderful friends Robbi Baskin, Rhonda Mackert, Stacey Brown, and John Blakemore for helping with the final editing of this delightful tale. Thank you, Irene Foster Torres and Patton Boyle, for your suggestions on the cover.

A very special 'THANK YOU' to all my amazing friends and family who loved and supported me during the creation of this book. I greatly valued all your input and ideas. You were always there for me whenever I needed you and often listened to me talk about the book for hours. I love you.

And last, but not least, a huge thank you to the Divine for sending me this story and helping me write it.

Author's Biography

GC Sinclaire loves to write and could not imagine her life without it. Her inspiration comes from many places. One of these sources is Sinclaire's vivid dreams. When she writes them down, more facts emerge, almost like she has lived them.

Just like 'Arianna - A Tale from the Eleven Kingdoms' and 'Mystic Highlands Love Story,' this latest novel is the result of one of these dreams. Several other stories, including sequels to her previous books, are in various stages of completion.

If you would like to read more about GC and her works, please visit her Facebook page, GC Sinclaire, or her web page at <u>www.gcsinclaire.com</u>. You can check on updates there and connect with the author.

www.ingramcontent.com/pod-product-compliance
Lightning Source LLC
Chambersburg PA
CBHW022100170626
46808CB00002B/520